I0538033

THE GEMINI RISING ROCKIN' MACHINE

BOOK FIVE: SIPHON YOUR MINDS & THE VEGETARIAN AND THE SLAUGHTERHOUSE

**Book Five: Siphon Your Minds &
The Vegetarian And The Slaughterhouse
Copyright 2014 by The Gemini Rising Rockin' Machine
ISBN-13: 978-0692306598 (Gemini Rising Rockin'
Machine, The)
ISBN-10: 0692306595**

For questions, comments you may send correspondence to.

thegeminirisingrockinmachine@twc.com.

**Official Website
www.thegeminirisingrockinmachine.com**

BOOK FIVE: SIPHON YOUR MINDS

Book Five: Siphon Your Minds (Pages 3-62)

(Side One) (Mind Messing With Side)
81. Siphon (300.)
82. Coma Made For Me (313.)
83. Dressed Up Like A Diner (240.)
84. Long Love Train Ride (249.)
85. Power To The Mammals Who Don't Walk On Two Legs (287.)

(Side Two) (Immortal & Celestial Beings Side)
86. Protector (182.)
(Opposites Attract And Create Life: 87-90)
87. The Entity Of Light (496.)
88. Lovely Heaven And Hated Hell (497.)
89. The Entity Of Darkness (498.)
90. Earth Like Planets Everywhere (499.)

(Side Three) (Dream & Death Side)
91. I Am Dream / Prelude To The Eye (80.)
92. Enjoy (The Eye) (33.)
93. Brave Face (166.)
94. I Can Smell Your Death (156.)
95. I Can Sense Your Death (157.)

(Side Four) (Cosmic Apocalyptic & Alien Side)
(The Three: 96-98)
96. Birth (208.)
97. Life (209.)
98. Death (210.)
(Double The Aliens = Double The Trouble: 99-100)
99. Crash Landed On Their Planet (583.) **(New)**
100. Humans In Space (584.) **(New)**

(Bonus Songs)
The Big Bang (266.)
Still Caught In A Dream (413.)
(New Cover Bonus Songs)
Never Have Sex With A Demon Trilogy: (863.-865.)

The Vegetarian And The Slaughterhouse (Pages 68-86)

The We In My Sleep (New Cover Bonus Story) (Pages 87-96)

81. Siphon

I was Born for Not-Around-Here
Coasting through Life
I'm-Kinda-Wild – I'm-Kinda-Dull
Still have Not-Found – My-Destination-Point
Knowing-Deep-Down-Inside
That-Something – Was-Hidden

Doing-My-Thing – One-Night
A-Spark was Awakened within Myself
I Keep it Lit-Bright by Feeding-It
My-Mind Rockin' ideas Every-Night
It has Stayed – Burning-Strong-Inside
As-I-Gobble-Them-Up – Chewing-Them
Just-Enough – So-I-Can – Spit-Them-Out
For-Them to Become Songs & Lyrical-Stories

(Chorus)
Lovers – Aliens – Monsters & Killers Are After Me
They Want Their-Secrets And Stories-Back
I-Siphoned Away – While They Were-Sleeping
Mind Rockin' – I'm Different
I'm A Siphon – Siphoning Out Things – That Dreamers
Never Want The Rest – Of The World To Know About

Now that I'm-Up to 300 – Mind-Rockers
I-Can – No-Longer-Ignore
The-Things that are Going-On
My-Dreams – Always-Wild and Intense
Are-Now – Acting like Hit-Men – Trying to
Take-Me-Out – While-I'm in Deep-Sleep
My-Punishment for My-Ability

My-Angry-Group of Dreaming-Executioners
Have had Enough of Me and My-Mind-Rockin'
In-My-Dreams – I've-Escaped – Burning and Drowning
Being-Swept into the Air by a Storm – Only to be Thrown
Back to the Ground – As-Hard as it Can,
I Heal – I Survive – I can Handle – My-Dreams

(Chorus)
Lovers – Aliens – Monsters & Killers Are After Me
They Want Their-Secrets And Stories-Back
I-Siphoned Away – While They Were-Sleeping
Mind Rockin' – I'm Different
I'm A Siphon – Siphoning Out Things – That Dreamers
Never Want The Rest – Of The World To Know About

Now as I-Write this Song titled Siphon
I'm-Thinking about a Dream that Woke
Me up Yesterday – Spitting – When-I told Myself
To-Spit it Out – The-Apple-Pie – For it's Poisoned
Looking-Up in the Dream that I was Having
Seeing the Sweet – Old-Lady that Gave-Me that Pie
Sitting in Her-Rocker on Her-Porch – Now a Demon

So with this Song-Siphon – I'm saying Good-Bye
To all Dreamers – Out-There – You're-Safe-Again
The Gemini Rising Rockin' Machine
Has left the Building – No-More – Mind-Rockin'
I and We – Will-Miss it a Lot – But we'll Survive
In a Song, a Dream or a Cold Hard Reality

(Chorus)
Lovers – Aliens – Monsters & Killers Are After Me
They Want Their-Secrets And Stories-Back
I-Siphoned Away – While They Were-Sleeping
Mind Rockin' – I'm Different
I'm A Siphon – Siphoning Out Things – That Dreamers
Never Want The Rest – Of The World To Know About

One more Thing – That-I'd like to Share
Is that I'm-Messing with Your-Minds
I-Hope-You had a Great-Time
As-I and We – Siphon-Your-Minds

Unknowingly at First – I thought my Mind Rockin' was Mine
Just Ideas and Stories – Inside-My-Mind – Now-I know Different
That-I'm-Different – I'm a Siphon – Siphoning out Things
That-Dreamers-Keep – Locked-Behind – Dream-Doors
Just in a Hope – They can Hide-Them from I-That is a We

82. Coma Made For Me

Wake-Up – Always the Same
Doing the Same-Things
Get-Up – Get-Dressed
Sit-Chained to a Table
Happens – Every-Day
Don't-Know-How or Why
It's – Making-Me-Crazy
From-Being – Driven-Insane

No-Matter how Hard – I-Try
This-Endless-Day – Will-Not-Go-Away
Lights-Come-On
I-Scream – Out-Loud
Looking at My – Closed-Door
With-No-way to Escape
As it Brings-Forth its Eternal
Hellish – Mental – Pains

(Chorus)
I Don't Have A Life
I Never Eat Or Drink
I Just Sit Here Endlessly
Hating The Life I'm Stuck With
That My Coma Made For Me

Hate-Having to Sit-Here – Having
One-Person after Another
Come into My-Room
Tell-Me their Problems – Then-Leave
Opening the Door – Just to be Replaced
By-Another – Same-Person – Again

I-See-Everyday at the Same-Time
Right-After the Person in Front of Them
Right-Before the Same-Person
That-Comes – After-Them
Every-Day – Knowing this Doesn't-Matter
'Cause-No-One is Allowed to Care
I'm-Just – There to Talk to
Never-Being – Allowed to be Heard

(Chorus)
I Don't Have A Life
I Never Eat Or Drink
I Just Sit Here Endlessly
Hating The Life I'm Stuck With
That My Coma Made For Me

Somebody out there Please
Pull the Damn-Plug – Already
I-Don't – Want to Live
Like this Anymore
These – Endless-Days
Of-Constant – Sameness
Never-Stop – Never-Change

People that Come
Into-My-Room – Every-Day
Cough and Sneeze on Cue
Laughing at the Same – Stupid-Jokes
They-Tell-Me at the Same-Time
The-Same-Stupid – Endless-Way

Acting-Like – I'm ok and Fine
Like-This is the First-Time to Them
Everything is Quite-Normal
As-I-Scream – Unnoticed – Unheard
In-All-Their – Same-Faces – That-I-Hate

(Chorus)
I Don't Have A Life
I Never Eat Or Drink
I Just Sit Here Endlessly
Hating The Life I'm Stuck With
That My Coma Made For Me

83. Dressed Up Like A Diner

The-Doorway – First-Appeared in 1968
Quite the Year for America
Lots of Pain – Lots of Love
Country was Hurting – Really-Bad
But in the Mist of That
Came this Doorway – Opening-Up
Inviting-People-Inside

It-Looked-Like an Ordinary-Diner
No-One-Thought – Anything-Different
As-They-Entered then Disappeared
Becoming the First-People
That was Allowed to Stay
Living-Forever – Eating-Apple-Pie

(Chorus)
What – Who Knows
It Is Real To The Touch
The Fountain Of Youth
Dressed Up Like A Diner
It Teases Me To Death
As I Live My Life – Trying To Find It

Born the Year the Doorway – Appeared
I-Felt-It – This-Doorway
Don't know How to Explain it
Other-Than it Left its Mark – On-Me
As-I – Grew-Older – I-Felt it More
Enticing-Me – Making-Me-Desire
Knowing – That it's Got-Me – Hooked

68-Diner – Gets-Really
Close to Me – Sometimes
Before-I-Can – Turn-Around
It's-Gone – All-That is Left
Is the Scent of a Sweet-Spring-Day
Making-Me-Know and Understand
I-Will-Be – Stuck in Endless-Winter

(Repeat Chorus)

Feeling the Doorway
It's – Very – Close
I – Just – Know
This-Time it's for Real
Figures the Doorway-Waited
'Til-I – Was in My-Forties
When-I was Already-Ready
Way-Back in My-Twenties

I-Go to My-Last-Time
Trying to Find-Forever
Feeling – Pretty – Good
Got some Stride in My-Walk
Ready to Force – My-Way
Into the Fountain of Youth

(Chorus)
What – Who Knows
It Is Real To The Touch
The Fountain Of Youth
Dressed Up Like A Diner
It Teases Me To Death
As I Live My Life – Trying To Find It

68-Diner – It's so Close
I-Feel-Like – I'm-Inside-It
But at Last – Damn-It
I-Can't – See it Once-Again
Walking-Away – Behind-Me it Appears
Shining a Very-Bright – Warm-Light

I-Stop – Walking
Afraid to Turn-Around
Slowly-I-Turn – There it Is
It's so Simple and Beautiful
Reaching for the Door – I-Scream
Seeing a Sign that Reads
Sorry – We're-Closed for Repairs
Try-Back – Sometime-Later
Maybe we'll Still be Here
For-Your – Dining-Needs

(Repeat Chorus)

84. Long Love Train Ride

We get Together – Every-Year
Reconnect with One-Another
This is So-Great – So-Freeing
We-All-Feel – Love and Warmth
Coming to Us – Like a Warm-Breeze

Ready – We-Close – Our-Eyes
Soak it In and Breathe it Out
So-Everyone – Can-Be as One – Together
We-Slowly-Open – Our-Eyes
Checking-Out – All the Smiling-Faces

(Chorus)
Once A Year – We Get It
The Long Love Train Ride
Once You Are Privileged
Enough – To Take Part In It
You'll Come Back Year After Year
For Some More Of The
Long Love Train Ride

There is No-Hate – Here
While this Train is Rolling
Even if You-Would – Want-It
It's-Impossible – It's-Not-Here

Hate – Does-Not-Exist
From Start to Finish
Only-Love and Fun is Offered
While-You're – Taking-Your-Ride
Wishing-Life was Always – Like-This

(Chorus)
Once A Year – We Get It
The Long Love Train Ride
Once You Are Privileged
Enough – To Take Part In It
You'll Come Back Year After Year
For Some More Of The
Long Love Train Ride

You-Know – When the Ride
Is-Almost-Over – You'll-Feel-It
The-Love-Sensations – Bathing-You
Start to Slip – Away from You – Slowly
By the Time – You-Get to the End
You're-Your – True-Self – Once-Again

With-All the Heavy of Day and Life
Waiting to Take – Their-Grip on You
Your-Soul – Once-Again – Will-Harden
For-True-Life – Is-No-Fantasy – It's the Real
You-Have to Live – Waiting-For
Next-Year's – Soul-Cleansing-Ride

(Chorus)
Once A Year – We Get It
The Long Love Train Ride
Once You Are Privileged
Enough – To Take Part In It
You'll Come Back Year After Year
For Some More Of The
Long Love Train Ride

(Chorus)
Once A Year – We Get It
The Long Love Train Ride
Once You Are Privileged
Enough – To Take Part In It
You'll Come Back Year After Year
For Some More Of The
Long Love Train Ride

85. Power To The Mammals Who Don't Walk On Two Legs

Another-Day – Another-Dollar
We-End-Them – Everyday
Our-Mammal – Earth-Brethren
Those that Don't-Walk on Two-Legs

Our-Own – Open-Targets
For the Killing-System
That-We – Mankind
Controls so Triumphantly
They-Don't – Stand a Chance
They-Cry as They-Die – Knowing-This

(Chorus)
Power To The Mammals
That Don't Walk On Two Legs
They Have No Voice
They Have No Choice
Mankind Should Give Them Both

These-Wonderful-Creatures – Love-Life
They-Don't – Want to Die
They-Live – Within their Own
Knowing – Which-Ones are the Hunters
Knowing – Which-Ones are the Prey

But the Equation of Man
In the Mix – Mixes it All-Up
Taking-Away – Their-Homes
With-Nowhere to Live – If-They-Live
Leaving – Them – Dead
Bringing-Them – Their-Doomsday – Every-Day

(Chorus)
Power To The Mammals
That Don't Walk On Two Legs
They Have No Voice
They Have No Choice
Mankind Should Give Them Both

Mother-Earth – In-Her-Own-Way
Knows-When a Species
Has had Enough of Dominance
Living on Her and With-Time
She-Starts to Change the Scene
Making it Very-Hard on the Powerful

Even with Everything in Us – Fighting
For-Our-Right to be Man and Woman
We will All – Eventually – Have to Sit-Back
With-Our – All-Knowing – Human-Minds
Watching a New – Better – More-Adaptable
Man and Woman of the Earth – Appear

(Chorus)
Power To The Mammals
That Don't Walk On Two Legs
They Have No Voice
They Have No Choice
Mankind Should Give Them Both

So-Bye-Bye – Two-Leggers
You-Were so Very-Bad
That – Mother-Earth – Decided
To make Us – Twin-Ones – Have
Four-Legs and Four-Arms – Instead

You – Two-Leggers – Think
That-You-Liked – Sex a Lot
You-Have – Nothing on Us
For-With – All-Our-Limbs
We-Can – Stay-Hooked-Up
For-Days – Enjoying-Ourselves
Laughing it Up – Forgetting – All-About-You

(Chorus)
Power To The Mammals
That Don't Walk On Two Legs
They Have No Voice
They Have No Choice
Mankind Should Give Them Both

86. Protector

Mother-Earth is Crying
She is In so Much-Pain
We-Just – Keep-On – Using-Her
Like-She is Not – The-One and Only
Beautiful-Planet in Our-Milky-Way

We-No-Longer – Care to be Known
As the Children of Earth
In the Back of Our-Minds
We-Know – This is a Lie
But-Life is so Constantly-Hard
We-Have to be Harder – Just to Live

The-Pain from Being-Pushed
Too-Fast to Death has Made
Mother-Earth – Cry with Anger

She just Wants to Keep-Living
Until-She – Dies-Naturally
Wanting this Pain to Stop
Mother-Earth – Makes-Her-Call

(Chorus)
Mother Earth – Has Called For Me
She Is No Longer – Just Slowly Dying
As Her Protector – I Come
Ready To Destroy – Her Enemies

Leaving – Mother-Earth with No-Choice
She-Has to do Something to Survive
Not-Being a Being – Just a Place
Where-Life – Can-Live its Life on
Left-Her with Only – One-Choice – I

As – Mother-Earth's – Protector
Without-Malice – Just-Certainty
I'm-Ready to Strike – My-First-Blow
Knowing it Will-Be – Devastating
Real-Big-Planet – Changing-One
I-Close-My-Eyes – To-My-Fury

I-Hear the Beautiful-Voice of
Mother-Earth – Telling-Me to Stop
I-Do – As-I-Am – Commanded to Do

I-Stand-There – An-Invisible-Giant
No-One on Earth – Can-See
Ready to Strike – Waiting-On-Her-Word

(Chorus)
Mother Earth – Has Called For Me
She Is No Longer – Just Slowly Dying
As Her Protector – I Come
Ready To Destroy – Her Enemies

Mother-Earth has Changed – Her-Mind
She-Loves – Her-Human-Children
She-Does-Not-Want – Them to Die
But-She – Will-No-Longer – Take-Their-Abuse
So-She-Pulls-Me – Back into Her to Ponder

Mother-Earth has Her-Answer
One-Hundred-Years – She's-Giving-Them
No-Time to Her at All
But to Them – It's the Difference
Between – Life and Death

(Chorus)
Mother Earth – Has Called For Me
She Is No Longer – Just Slowly Dying
As Her Protector – I Come
Ready To Destroy – Her Enemies

As-Mother-Earth's – New-Living-Protector
I-Will be Born from Within-Her
Ready to do My-Part – Helping-Mankind – Evolve
So-They-Can-Live – As-One with the Earth
Or – Ready to Destroy them All – If-They
Don't-Get – Their-Heads – Out of Their-Asses

(Chorus)
Mother Earth – Has Called For Me
She Is No Longer – Just Slowly Dying
As Her Protector – I Come
Ready To Destroy – Her Enemies
15

(Opposites Attract And Create Life 87-90)

87. The Entity Of Light

Before – Time – Began
All there Was – Was a
Void of Nothingness
In an Endless-Space
That-Nothing-Lived-In

Time had No-Meaning
It's – Never – Mattered
Then the Moment – Happened
Something-Appeared
Now in Endless-Nothingness
There is First-Light

(Chorus)
Let There Be Life
The Entity Of Light
Has Taken Form
Mother Maker
Is Ready To Create Creation

A-Cosmic – Gemini-Blast
Gave-Birth to First-Life
When-She-Opened – Her-Eyes
Nothing but Nothingness
Was-All that She – Could-See

The-First – Emotion-Created
Was-Sadness – With-Tears-Falling
Mother-Maker – Kept-Crying
Creating-Stars with Each-Tear
Until the Dawn of the Entity of Darkness

(Chorus)
Let There Be Life
The Entity Of Light
Has Taken Form
Mother Maker
Is Ready To Create Creation

88. Lovely Heaven And Hated Hell

Mother-Maker is so Happy
Her-Sadness has Created – Wonderment
But-Something is Not-Quite – Right
Something is Missing
So-More –Tears are Shed

Mother-Maker – Stretches-Out
Contemplating – Enjoying – Looking at All
The-Singular – Suns and Stars
That-Stretch-Out – As-Far as She – Can-See
Still-Sadness – Will-Not-Leave-Her – Alone

(Chorus)
Mother Maker
Is Our Lovely Heaven
Father Un-maker
Is Our Hated Hell
Hand And Hand Together
They Created Life

Watching in the Nothingness
Is Our-Father – Un-maker
That was Born at the Same-Time
From the Same Cosmic – Gemini-Blast
That-Born-Mother-Maker

When-He-Opened – His-Eyes
He-Liked the Nothingness
It-Felt like Home to him
When-He-Turned -Around
He-Saw – Mother-Maker
Creating a Creation that He-Hated
So-He-Sank-Back – Into the Darkness
Waiting for Her – To-Tire – Herself-Out

(Chorus)
Mother Maker
Is Our Lovely Heaven
Father Un-maker
Is Our Hated Hell
Hand And Hand Together
They Created Life
17

89. The Entity Of Darkness

Many-Years in Waiting
Father-Un-maker is Ready
Hard to Remember The Brief
Moment of Happiness
He was Allowed to Feel
Before it was Replaced with Hate

First-Sight of All the Ugly
Small-Lights that Mother-Maker
Created-Out of Her-Sadness
Her-Beauty – Stirred-Something – Inside-Him
Like-He-Had to Have-Her-Forever

(Chorus)
Let There Be No Light
The Entity Of Darkness
Has Taken Form
Father Un-Maker
Is Ready To Un-Create Life

Timing is Perfectly-Wrong
For-Father-Un-maker's – Plan
He does not Know, his Impatience
Will Ruin what he most Desires
The Destruction of Everything
That Mother Maker Created

Waiting for So-Long
Hating and Wanting – All-Alone
Is the Opposite-Effect – He had in Mind
As the Time of Dawn is About to Be
Created a Few-Years – After
He-Stepped – Out of the Nothingness

(Chorus)
Let There Be No Light
The Entity Of Darkness
Has Taken Form
Father Un-Maker
Is Ready To Un-Create Life

Mother-Maker is Lying-Down
She is so Tired from Crying
So-Hard for so Many-Years
Never-Having to Worry-About
Anything but Sadness
Never made Her-Wonder
If-There is Someone-Else
To-Spend – Her-Loneliness with

Out of the Nothingness that Still-Exists
She-Senses – Another Like Her
Completely – Opposite of Her
She-Stands – Back-Up and Smiles
So-Happy that She is No-Longer – Alone
Happiness-Turns to Fear
As-Father-Un-maker – Shows-His-Fangs

(Chorus)
Let There Be No Light
The Entity Of Darkness
Has Taken Form
Father Un-Maker
Is Ready To Un-Create Life

Father-Un-maker – Soars so Fast
Taking-Hold of Mother-Maker
So-Easily because of Her-Weakness
With-Huge-Fangs – Ready to Strike
He-Takes-Them and Sinks-Them
Deep-Into – Her-Curvy-Form

The-Pleasure – The-Pain – Makes-Her
Move-Around with Such-Force
She-Makes – Her-Creations
Spin-Around and Smash into Each-Other
Making-Them-Combine – To-Make – Living-Planets

(Chorus)
Let There Be No Light
The Entity Of Darkness
Has Taken Form
Father Un-Maker
Is Ready To Un-Create Life

90. Earth Like Planets Everywhere

Surprise – Loneliness – Mixed with Lust
Brought-Forth the Marriage of
Mother-Maker and Father-Un-maker
They-Both-Loved and Hated the Other
The-Deep – Imbedded-Need – Not to be Alone
Made-Them – Use the Other for Their-Needs

Making-Love not Paying -Attention
For-Many – Billions of Years
A-Lot can Happen – When-You – Finally-Notice
What-Happened to the Universe that is You
Life on Blue-Green-Red and Orange-Planets
Everywhere to be Seen – Flourishing so Bright

(Chorus)
Earth Like Planets Everywhere
Is No Way For Life To Be Lived
There Can Be Only One Per Group
So Neighboring Distant Planets
Can Not Search For The Meaning Of Life

Amazement with Love is What
Mother-Maker – Felt and Saw
Disgust with Hate is What
Father-Un-maker Felt and Saw

Mother-Maker – Danced-Around so Happy
Father-Un-maker – Stomped-Around so Angry
Mother-Maker is So-Surprised
She-Wants to Create – Even more Planets
Father-Un-maker is So-Surprised
He-Wants to Destroy – All the Planets

(Chorus)
Earth Like Planets Everywhere
Is No Way For Life To Be Lived
There Can Be Only One Per Group
So Neighboring Distant Planets
Can Not Search For The Meaning Of Life

With-Mighty-Hands – Father-Un-maker
Scoops-Up and Swallows
Hundreds of Planets that He-Hates
Mother-Maker in Shock
Stops-Dancing and Tries to Stop-Him

With-Love – Within-His-Being
For-Mother-Maker
Father-Un-maker – Stops and Stands-Still
Mother-Maker is So-Mad – That-Her
Scream – Destroys even More-Planets

Father-Un-maker – Laughs and Tells
Mother-Maker to Keep on Screaming
So-She can Destroy – All the Planets for Him
So-He – Doesn't-have to Taste that Foul
After-Taste that Comes from Eating-Planets

(Chorus)
Earth Like Planets Everywhere
Is No Way For Life To Be Lived
There Can Be Only One Per Group
So Neighboring Distant Planets
Can Not Search For The Meaning Of Life

After many Years of Talking and Making-Love
Mother-Maker and Father-Un-maker
Come to a Forever – Agreement
Only-One-Planet in a Group – Can have Life
All-Other-Planets – Around it will Never
Be-Allowed to Have – Any-Life-Forever

Father-Un-maker holds Mother-Maker
After-One-More – Great-Big-Kiss
He-Makes – One more Proclamation
That if a Living-Planet – Dies
Or the Life that Lives on a Planet
Kills this Planet for Power
Then that Group of Planets
Will be Ate-Up by Him – For-His-Fiber

(Repeat Chorus)

91. I Am Dream / Prelude To The Eye

(Spoken)
If-I-Think for I-Am is the Positive
Then-I-Dream for I-Am-Not
Has to Be the Negative
Without-Life – We cannot Dream – And
We cannot Live – If-We do Not-Dream

(Dream)
I am Dream – Go to Sleep
Release-Your-Mind
Have some Fun
Scare the Hell – Out of yourself
I – Don't – Care
I-Am-Just-Here
Your-Outlet to Use – As-You
Fill or Release – Yourself

I am Dream – Go to Sleep
Release-Your-Mind
I've-Been-Around – Since-Day-Two
I am Not – Alive like You
I am a Pure – Power of Energy
Created as an Escape
For-All the Enlightened
Minds of the Universe

I am Dream – Go to Sleep
Release-Your-Mind
I-Can-Not-Promise to Protect-You
You – Are on Your-Own
Where-You-Choose to Go
Is-All-Up to You
If-You can Keep-Control
Maybe-You can Stay-Clear
Of the Eye of the Nightmare

(Spoken - The Eye Enters The Dreamer)
Dream stays Silent – Watching the Eye – Enter the Dreamer
This-Nightmare-Entity – Has-Come to Feed
Dream has No-Need to Even-Think – About the Dreamer
There are so Many-Dreamers and He is Just-One of Them

(The Eye)
Sleep-Tight - Open-Your-Mind-Up
Give-Me – Your-Nightmares
You will Feed-Me as I-Eat-Up
All-Your – Fears and Tears
While-You-Feel – My-Painful-Energy
Soaking in You – All the Way to Your-Soul

(The Dreamer)
No-Way – This cannot Be-Happening
I-Feel so Very-Weird
Like-You are Trying to Take – My-Will
Tempting-Me with Force – To let You-In

(The Eye)
That's-Right – Ha Ha
However-Twit – You are Mistaken
You-Dreaming-Fool
I-Do-Not-Need – Your-Permission
To-Enter-Your-Mind

I am Already-Here in Your
Mental – Dreaming – Cobwebs
I-Just-Want – You to Comply
Sooner than Later
I-Want to Feed
Feast on Your-Nightmares
I-Sensed-You from Afar

Your-Tasty – Mental-Waves
Were-Calling – Out to Me
So-Strong – They-Were
I – Released – Thousands
From-My – Nightmare-Grasp
Just so I – Could-Enjoy!
Your – Delicious – Smelling
Subconscious – All by Itself

Now – Nightmare-Now for Me
I'm so Hungry – I'm-Salivating
I-Want to Feed – Off of You so Deep
That-My-Force will Scar – Your-Soul

23

The almost fully into Dreaminess, Dreamer screams no, already
knowing that it will do no good. The Dreamer also knows that it is up
to him to survive The Eye's temptations. So with one last thought
going through his Mind the Dreamer focuses himself right before he
fully surrenders to deep Sleep. And that last thought are the words,
Power = Freedom.

(The Dreamer)
I-Grab-Hold of a Lightning-Bolt
To-Escape from the Huge
Nightmare in the Sky
It-Laughs and Snaps its Teeth
Using the Sky to Soar after Me

Look-Back – Losing a Little-Focus
My-Lightning-Bolt – Starts to Shrink
I'm-Holding on to Barely-Anything
As-I – Start to Panic

(Chorus)
Calmness – I Can Not Give Up
Calmness – Is My Power
Calmness – Is My Safety Zone
Calmness – Will Lead Me To Freedom

Soaked to the Bone
Gray-Skies be Gone
As-Only – My-Fingertips
Are-Grasping – My-Lightning-Bolt

Smiling in Blue-Skies
As a Rainbow-Appears
If-I – Time this Just-Right
As-I – Fall onto It – Sliding-Down
The-Nightmare in the Sky
Will-Pass-Me – Hungrily-By

(Chorus)
Calmness – I Can Not Give Up
Calmness – Is My Power
Calmness – Is My Safety Zone
Calmness – Will Lead Me To Freedom

Look-Up – No-Fright in Sight
My-Mind is Relaxing
As-I – Look-Ahead at My-Ride
Across – Warm – Lovely – Colors

Dreaming so Free and Easy-Now
Realizing in Horror a Mountain-Side
Is-Where – My-Rainbow-Ride – Ends
Taking the Dreaming-Pain
As-I-Jump – Off-My-Rainbow
Landing-Nice and Soft on Tall –Purple-Grass

(Chorus)
Calmness – I Can Not Give Up
Calmness – Is My Power
Calmness – Is My Safety Zone
Calmness – Will Lead Me To Freedom

I'm-Ok – I'm-Fine
Standing in This-Field of Purple-Grass
Wind-Begins to Blow so Hard
That its Speed is Making the Grass-Sing
Calming at First – Then with a Touch of Evil
The-Tall-Purple-Grass – Starts to Scream in Pain

In the Distance is a Beautiful
Evil-Lady – Staring at Me
She-Smiles and Spreads-Her-Arms
Now – She is Wearing a Black-Cloak
Chanting-Something – I can't Understand

Growling and Howling – Replaces the Wind's-Fury
As-Giant-Beasts – Start to be Born – From-Out of Her-Cloak
With-Hunger in Their-Blood – Red-Eyes
They-Start to Run – Towards-Me in Rage
Wanting to Eat-Me-Up – Alive

(Chorus)
Calmness – I Can Not Give Up
Calmness – Is My Power
Calmness – Is My Safety Zone
Calmness – Will Lead Me To Freedom

(The Eye Re-Enters The Dream)

(The Eye)
That's-More-Like-It
Finally a Proper – Bloody-Nightmare
For-Me to Sink – My-Teeth-In
I-Want – More-Flesh
I-Want – More-Blood
Bigger-Chunks and Deeper-Buckets
Nightmare – Even-Harder for Me

(The Dreamer)
Go-Away – You are Ruining – My-Dreams
Go-Bother – Someone-Else
Leave-Me in Peace
I've had Enough of You

(The Eye)
What is That – You-Say to Me
You-Foolish – Weak-Dreamer

(The Dreamer)
You-Heard-Me – Eye
No-More-Nightmares from You
Leave-My-Dreams and Let-Me-Be

(The Eye)
I-Am the Eye
Nightmares – Belong to Me
You have No-Choice – Any-More
I'm-Embedded – Inside-You – 'Til-Forevermore
Your-Only-Peace will be When-You-Awake

(The Dreamer)
Hell with it Then – If-You won't Go-Away
I'll just Wake-Up and Rid-Myself of You
(Wake-Up – Wake-Up – Wake-Up)

(The Eye)
Foolish – Dreaming – Twit
I'll just Wait – 'Til-Tomorrow-Night
Make-You – Nightmare even Harder
Ha Ha Ha

92. Enjoy (The Eye)

(The Dreamer)
My-Dreaming-Controller
The-Eye of the Nightmare
Commands-Me to Sleep
Early and Extra-Long
Each and Every-Night

I-Damn – His-Command
Daring-Myself to Stay-Awake
I'm so Tired – All the Time
At-Least – I-Own-These-Hours
I-Do-Not – Even-Enjoy
Knowing-I'll – Finally-Collapse
Into-Another – Night-Full of
Endless – Damnable – Nightmares

I-Hate – My-Life
I'd-Trade-My-Life
With an Insane-Person
I-Believe that I-Could
Conquer-Over-Insanity
From – My-Years of Battling
The-Eye of the Nightmare

(Chorus)
Night After Night I'm Attacked
By Every Nightmare
That The Eye Can Invent For Me
I Fight – Injustice
I Destroy – Tyranny
I Kill Evil
I Get Stronger And Smarter
As The Years Pile Up
So I Can Take Over
And Devour The Eye

Punishment – I-Receive
For-My-Will of Freedom
Is-Fierce and Mighty
With-Lots and Lots of
Sharp-Teeth – Biting-Me
All the Way – Down to My-Soul

The-Eye – His – Kick-Back-Name
Is so Single-Minded
That-No-Heed or Concern
Is-Ever – Shown-My-Way
I get Stronger – Every-Night
Waiting – Biding-My-Time
As the Eye – Feeds-Off – My-Nightmares

Show – Weakness and Uncertainty
Makes-The-Eye – Stop-His-Feeding
So-He – Can-Save-My-Life
Before-I-Hit the Ground – or Get
Completely-Swallowed-Up

After-Wards – He-Laughs –Hard and Evil
Certain of His-Strength – Over-Me
Look-Away – Grinding-My-Teeth
Invisibly – Beating-My-Fist
Against – My-Powerful-Chest

(Chorus)
Night After Night I'm Attacked
By Every Nightmare
That The Eye Can Invent For Me
I Fight – Injustice
I Destroy – Tyranny
I Kill Evil
I Get Stronger And Smarter
As The Years Pile Up
So I Can Take Over
And Devour The Eye

(Chorus)
Night After Night I'm Attacked
By Every Nightmare
That The Eye Can Invent For Me
I Fight – Injustice
I Destroy – Tyranny
I Kill Evil
I Get Stronger And Smarter
As The Years Pile Up
So I Can Take Over
And Devour The Eye

(The Eye)
Go to Sleep – My-Dreaming-Fool
Nightmare for Me – Another-Time
Enjoy as I-Seep – Back in Deep
Enjoying-More – Bloody-Destruction

That-Only-I – The-Eye
With-My – Nightmarish-Wonderfulness
Can-Make-You – Enjoy-Once-Again
Making-You-Scream for More
While-You're – Always-Pleading
Deep – Down – Inside
For-Me to Stop – Torturing-You

I-Never-Will – You're-My-Meal
I-Love-Feeding – Off-Your-Mind
You and About a Million-More
Is-All that I-Need – Every-Day
To-Stay so Mighty and Strong

(Chorus)
I Am The Eye Of The Nightmare
I've Been Around Since Day Three
I Will Always Exist
For I Am Pure Force Of Power
That Can Never Die

Go to Sleep – My-Dreaming-Fool
Nightmare for Me – Another-Time
Enjoy as I-Seep – Back in Deep
Enjoying-More – Bloody-Destruction

(Chorus)
I Am The Eye Of The Nightmare
I've Been Around Since Day Three
I Will Always Exist
For I Am Pure Force Of Power
That Can Never Die

(The Eye)
Enjoy – This-Trip's for You
Scream and Bleed
Laugh and Cry
Enjoy – You will Love-It
Terrified with Ecstasy
Loved with Hate
Your-Mind – Will-Melt
From the Fear of Wanting-It

Enjoy – It's-All for You
Go-Ahead – Starve and Feast
Go-Ahead – Fly or Fall
You-Hate-Able – Good-ling
Enjoy – You-Need-This
Go-Ahead – Kiss and Bite
Go-Ahead – Peace and Death
You-Love-Able – Sick-Ling

Enjoy – You're-Finally-Up to the Climax
You have Shaken with Delight
You have Cringed with Acceptance
You have Teared at Your-Flesh
Eating-Up the Falling-Pieces

Enjoy – The-End is Almost-Here
Not so Crystal-Clear is It
It's-More of a Fiery-Frozen-Rainbow
A-Beautiful-Butterfly with Wings
That-Have the Sharpest of Blades
That-Cuts – Your-Mind to Shredded-Clay

Enjoy – As-You – Start to Awake
From-Your – Secret-Desire
Don't-Forget the Snake in a Cradle
That is One-Great – Create
To-Make-You – Love and Hate – Yourself

Enjoy – You have Earned-This
The-Sweet and The-Sour
The-Unglamorous – Glamor
The-Thorn in Hand
With a Terrifying – Peace of Mind

Enjoy - You have Tasted up
All the Sweet-Excess
While-Gorged-Down – Unhappily
All of its Mad-Drippings

Enjoy – You are Happy and Helpless
The-End is Sliced-Up so Nice
It has Pierced-You – Making-You-Smile
While-Biting – Your-Tongue – Bloody
You're-About to Soar
You're-About to Score
You're-About-To

(The Dreamer)
Waking-Up – The-Eye – Tells-Me
As-I was Drifting-Back
I-Not-Fully-Giving it My-All
I'm-Messing-Up the Flow
For-His-Need for Feed
On-My-Cosmic – Mental-Waves
Which-Makes-Him – Whole and Full
So-I'm-To – Love-To
Nightmare – Every-Night

(Chorus)
I Am The Dreamer
I've Been Around Since Day Four
I Am Forever Damned
For All I Ever Dream
Are Things That I Don't Want
And Never Things That I Need

I Must Suffer Through
To The Eye I Must Be True
I Must Enjoy Myself
Feeding The Eye Of The Nightmare
The Eye Is My Comfortable Doom
So I Enjoy – Enjoy – Enjoy
Myself Nightmaring All Night Long

(Repeat Chorus)

31

93. Brave Face

I-Wake – Do-My-Things
Then-I-Put-On – My-Brave-Face
Stop at My – Exit-Door
Take a Deep-Breath
Grab the Knob – Turn-It
Letting in All the Out

Walking – I-Feel-Calm
Doing this All the Time
Makes-Me be Myself
The-One – Who-Walks by
Watching and Listening
To-Everything-Around
Keeping it All to Myself

Nine-Steps is All there Is
Just-Walk – Right-Down-Them
I'm on the Sidewalk
The-In is Now – Amongst the Out
Not-Paid-Attention to – As-Usual
I'm the Ghost that Everybody-Sees
But-Nobody – Wants to Know

(Chorus)
Brave Face Is What I Have
I'm Alone But Doing Fine
Don't Think I Need You
To Help Make My Day

(Chorus)
Brave Face Is What I Have
I'm Alone But Doing Fine
Don't Think I Need You
To Help Make My Day

Walking by Untouched
Stopping to Notice
The-Not-Interesting
The-I – Just-Did-Thats
All-Do-Their-Best
To-Be – So-Boring
So-Funny and So-Bloody

They-Entertain-Me
With-Nothing and Everything
If the Nothings and the Everythings
Decided to Take a Close-Look
They-Would-Find the In to Their-Out

A-Puppeteer – Controlling-Their-Lives
Doing-Nothing – While-Walking-By
Everything – While-Stopping-By
So-Quick of a Stop – I-Have
That-No-One – Will-Ever-See-Me
As-I-Walk-Away – Not-Ever-Being-There

(Chorus)
Brave Face Is What I Have
I'm Alone But Doing Fine
Don't Think I Need You
To Help Make My Day

(Chorus)
Brave Face Is What I Have
I'm Alone But Doing Fine
Don't Think I Need You
To Help Make My Day

33

94. I Can Smell Your Death

Wherever-I-Go – It's the Same
The-Pain of Someone's – Dying
Comes-Up to Me
Slapping-Me in My-Mind
Kicking-Me in My-Guts
My-Gift – Is a Damn-Curse
I – Can – Smell – Death
It-Does-Not – Smell-Sweet

A-Lot of Times the Person
Does-Not – Even-Know
That-Very-Soon – They-Will-Get-Sick
Living the Last-Days – They-Have-Left
In-Nothing but Constant-Pain
After-That – Their-Slow-Death

Death –Telling so Many
Damn-Same-Reactions
Received from All of Them
Is-Hate and Hostility – or
A -Pleading for Help
From a Fearful – Dying-Person

Never-Knowing – What-I-Will-Do
Is-Constantly – On-My-Mind
Do-I – Just-Keep-Walking
Should-I-Stop and Tell-Them

(Chorus)
I Can Smell Your Death
Hurts Me So Deep Down Inside
That I Can't Help You
I Just Tell You That
You're Going To Die Soon
As Everyone's Death
Is Slowly Killing Me Later

(Repeat Chorus)

Even though I-Try to Stay-Hard
Even after All –These-Long-Years
I-Have to Help – Good-People-Out
Telling-Them of Their – Coming Deaths
Letting-Them-Stop – What-They are Doing
And-Start to Live for the Day

It-Tears-Out – Pieces of My-Soul
When-I-Tell-Parents the Terrible-News
What is Happening to Their-Child
That-They – Don't have Much-Time-Left
Not to Waste-Time
Thinking about Future-Tomorrows
Only-Precious – Few-Moments
Of-What is Left of Their – Child's-Life

Never-Knowing if My-Efforts
Are-Ever – Needed or Not
Do – I – Do – Any – Good
Maybe by Easing some Pains
By-Telling – Someone of Their-Death
I-Put-Them – Right-Where
Death – Wants-Them to Be

I'll-Probably – Never-Know
I-Don't-Think – I-Want to Either
I-Guess – I'm Just – Some-Kinda
Messenger of Death's-Tool
That-Death has Made to Use
Making it Easier on the Dying
Or – Use as a Fear for the Dying
For-Them to Die – Even-Faster

(Chorus)
I Can Smell Your Death
Hurts Me So Deep Down Inside
That I Can't Help You
I Just Tell You That
You're Going To Die Soon
As Everyone's Death
Is Slowly Killing Me Later

(Repeat Chorus)

Becoming-Famous was Not-My-Intent
It just Happened – One-Day
My-Face was Everywhere
Word got Out on What – I-Could-Do
Now-Everybody – Wants-Me
To-Smell-Them for Death
Coming-Up to Me in Droves
Weakening-Me to Sickness

I-Can't-Eat – I-Can't-Sleep
Pleading as They – Show-Me
With-Tears in Their-Eyes
Pictures of Their – Loved-Ones
Too-Much – Way too Fast – Coming at Me
Sends-Me into a Panic-Attack
Running-Away – Fearing for My-Health
Starting to Feel – Closer to My own Death

Running as Far as I-Can
Away from My-Nightmare
Does-No-Good at All
Get-Tired – Stop-Running
Turn-Around – They-Found-Me
Then it Starts – All-Back up Again

Consuming-My-Being – With-Their-Deaths
This-Time – There are Way too Many
In-No-Time at All – I'm-Completely-Sick
Knowing this by Smelling it On-Myself
My-Dying is Coming to Me – Very-Quickly
I -Give-Up and Try to Find a Peaceful-Spot
Where-I-Can – Lay-Down by Myself and Die-Alone

(Chorus)
I Can Smell Your Death
Hurts Me So Deep Down Inside
That I Can't Help You
I Just Tell You That
You're Going To Die Soon
As Everyone's Death
Is Slowly Killing Me Later

(Repeat Chorus)

95. I Can Sense Your Death

Wherever – I – Go
Whoever-I-Run-Into
It's-Always the Same
Their-Death-Date – Comes to Me
Telling-Me – When-They're-Going to Die

It's-Like – I-Sense in My-Mind
Invisible-Markings on Them
Of-How-Many-Days
They have Left to Live
Before – Mr. Death – Comes for them

Yes-I-Can – Help-You
Just-Make an Appointment
I-Am a Very – Busy-Person
There-Are so Many in the Need
Knowing the Actual-Day
They are Going to Die
You-Might have to Wait-Awhile
There-Will be Many in Front of You

Tell-Me – What is Your-Price
What is Your-Death-Date – Worth
Reach in Deep – You-Tight-Wads
Give it to Me – 'Til it Makes
You-Feel that You are Bleeding

(Chorus)
Pay Me Very Quickly
I Can Sense Your Death
If You Want The Heads Up
You Better Open Up
Your Wallets Very Wide
So My Greedy Thick Fingers
Can Fit Nicely Deep Inside Them

(Repeat Chorus)

Wherever – Whoever
It's-Always the Same-Old-Same
New-Person is so Important
So-Rich and Very-Powerful
They-Have to Show it Off

I-Get a Mr. Big-Bucks
Pulling-Out – His-Wallet
Flashing it Around for All to See
Trying to Show – How-Much-Their
Wealthy – Dominance is Worth

My-Court – My-Backyard
My-Rules – My-Price – Prices-Vary
Drastically – More-Money-You-Have
More – Money – Your
Death-Date – Will-Cost-You

I-Love the Power-I-Receive
When-I-Keep-Telling – Mr. Big-Bucks – No
'Til the Price is So-High and Unfair
He-Gives it to Me-Shaking
With-His-Face – Red-With-Anger

What-Choice – Do-I-Give-Them
They-Can – Go on Not-Knowing
Lusting-Over – Living -Their-Lives
Then-One-Day – Very-Soon – They-Die
Start-Hearing-That-Big
Cash-Register in the Sky
Making the Sound of No-Sale
With-Their-Last-Thoughts – Being
I – Could – Have – Known

(Chorus)
Pay Me Very Quickly
I Can Sense Your Death
If You Want The Heads Up
You Better Open Up
Your Wallets Very Wide
So My Greedy Thick Fingers
Can Fit Nicely Deep Inside Them
(Repeat Chorus)

Wherever – Whoever
It's-Always the Same-Old-Same
New-Person is so Important
Because-They – Help-People-Out
They are Needed so Much
That the World – Can't go on Without-Them
I-Have to Give-Them the Best-Deal
Because-They are Good and Most-Deserving

Good for You but You-Being-Good
Does not Help – Pay-My-Bills
I-Have-Some – Very-Big-Bills
All-Due to the Life-I-Live
I-Deserve-It – It is Hell on Me
Living-Life – Knowing only Death

I-Could-Give-Them – Their-Date for Free
But that Makes – No-Sense to Me
What-I-Have to Offer
Is-Priceless to Them
And a Big-Pain in My-Being

So-Don't be Fooled into Believing
By the Others that Tell-You
I-Am a Fake – By-Giving-Me – Your-Money
Nothing is All – You'll-get For Your-Trouble

I-Want-Your-Money – That is True
Even-More – Than-You-Can-Afford
Trust-Me – I'm-Telling-You the Truth
When-I-Tell-You – You-Will-Die
On the Day – I-Tell-You – You-Are
Unless-You – Save-Yourself from Your-Death

(Chorus)
Pay Me Very Quickly
I Can Sense Your Death
If You Want The Heads Up
You Better Open Up
Your Wallets Very Wide
So My Greedy Thick Fingers
Can Fit Nicely Deep Inside Them
(Repeat Chorus)

39

96. Birth

Stars are Aligned
The-Time has Arrived
Destiny and Fate – Have-Been
Waiting for This for So-Long
The-Birth of a Special-Child
The-One that Changes-Everything

Whose-Three will Be the Key
That-Sets-Them – Free
No-More will They – Have to go On
Doing-What – Eternity and Infinity
Programmed – Them to Do for So-Long

(Chorus)
I Was Born For Greatness
Destiny And Fate Had A Plan
They Got Together And Made My Birth
One For Only The Stars To Know
Putting Me Above Everyone Else

The-Birth of I – Means the End
No-More-Children – Will be Born
The-World – Will-Be in Turmoil
So – Many – People
Having the Same-Questions
Why – How – How-Many
Can-You – Save-Us
Waiting for the Big-Answers
Never-Getting – Even-One – Honest-One

Last-One to Be-Born
Right-Before-Me – Was the Very
Last-One to Have – Either
A-Destiny or Fate
Planned-Out for Them
For-Me – I'm the First
And-Only – That was Ever
Allowed to Be-Able to Have
Both at the Same-Time

40

(Chorus)
I Was Born For Greatness
Destiny And Fate Had A Plan
They Got Together And Made My Birth
One For Only The Stars To Know
Putting Me Above Everyone Else

The-Child that Was-Born
A few Hours – Before-Me
Will get All the Attention
They will Look to Her for Answers
Since all Will-Believe –She is the Very
Last – Child
That was Born on Planet-Earth

Never-Knowing about I
The – Birth – Unnoticed
I-Will be Raised by the Two
Who-Were the Only-Chosen
To-Know about My-Birth
And-What-My-Life
Means to this World

They-Gave-Me so Much-Love
For-They – Loved-Me so Much
Just like I – Belonged to Them
I-Was the Answer to Their-Prayers
They-Raised-Me as Their-Son
Never-Letting-Me-Know or
Telling-Me of My-Path

(Chorus)
I Was Born For Greatness
Destiny And Fate Had A Plan
They Got Together And Made My Birth
One For Only The Stars To Know
Putting Me Above Everyone Else

97. Life

I was Sent-Away to School
Learned so Much so Very-Fast
There was Nothing – That was Beyond-Me
I-Wanted to Know about Something
I'd-Find-It and Absorb-It-In
There it Stayed to Remember-Forever

I-Knew – I was Different
This-Bothered-Me – I-Loved-It
I – Found – Out – Nobody
Could-Do what I-Could-Do
If-There was Someone out There
That had Something I Needed

I-Searched them Out and Took-Away
What-They-Had – What-I-Wanted
Keeping it for Myself
Leaving-Them with Nothing

(Chorus)
My Life is so Great and Grand
I'm Always right
Never am I wrong
I've Grabbed a Hold of Life
Taken what I Wanted from it
Never feeling Regret for What I did

After-Graduation – Everybody-Wanted-Me
I-Had the Highest – Test-Scores-Ever
Dubbed the Smartest-Man – Who-Ever-Lived
They-Come to Me-Begging to Work for Them
Especially the Government

(Chorus)
My Life Is So Great And Grand
I'm Always Right
Never Am I wrong
I've Grabbed A Hold Of Life
Taken What I Wanted From It
Never Feeling Regret For What I Did

42

Most felt I was the Key to their Answers
If Anyone could Change what was Happening
I was the best Solution to the Problem
I was offered Everything I needed
No Price was too Much to Save them

I did my Best - I did my Damnedest
Coming up with only Nothing
Got real Uncaring, still Nothing
Then I got real Evil, single Life
Did not Matter, had no Meaning
If I was to Save the whole World

(Chorus)
My Life Is So Great And Grand
I'm Always Right
Never Am I wrong
I've Grabbed A Hold Of Life
Taken What I Wanted From It
Never Feeling Regret For What I Did

People Volunteered by the Thousands
Losing Count on how Many I used Up
They Expired, then were Put in a Body bag
Time - Hard Work - & Greed = Discovery
I was on to Something very Big now
Telling the World to Hold their Breath
As I Plunged into Human DNA my Cure

Exhausted, I picked Myself up
Telling the World I had Nothing
I Failed, There Is No Answer
There Is No Cure For Mankind
No Matter what I try
The only Answer is No

(Chorus)
My Life Is So Great And Grand
I'm Always Right
Never Am I wrong
I've Grabbed A Hold Of Life
Taken What I Wanted From It
Never Feeling Regret For What I Did

I-Stopped-Working – I-Started-Back
Then-One-Day – Out of Nowhere
Something so Grand and Special
Came to Me – All of a Sudden
I-Had-It – I-Knew-What – I-Had to Do

Finally-Getting the Answer
After so Many-Years – I was So-Pumped
After-This – I-Would – Own the World
Keeping-It to Myself this Time
Telling-No-One of My-Discovery
Entering-My-Lab – I-Felt-like a God

(Chorus)
My Life Is So Great And Grand
I'm Always Right
Never Am I wrong
I've Grabbed A Hold Of Life
Taken What I Wanted From It
Never Feeling Regret For What I Did

Another-Failure and Success
I-Had the Answer – That was True
But it Was-One – That-Was so Devastating
I will Never – Allow-Myself to Tell-It
Finding-Out – Through a Horrible-Surprise

I-Am the Carrier
I-Am the Reason-Why
I'm-Living-Death to the World
My-Birth is the Bomb
My-Life is the Fuse
My-Death will Be the Spark

(Chorus)
My Life Is So Great And Grand
I'm Always Right
Never Am I wrong
I've Grabbed A Hold Of Life
Taken What I Wanted From It
Never Feeling Regret For What I Did

98. Death

Stopped-Worrying – About the World
Bought-Myself an Island
Filled it With – More-Women
Than-I-Had the Time to Enjoy
I-Lived-My-Life – Like a King
Wanting for Nothing – Having-Everything

Every-Day – Picking-Four or Five-Women
To-Spend the Day with Their-King
Doing-Whatever-I-Wanted
My-Queens – They-Lived-Marvelous
Inside a Protected-Paradise
Far-Away From the World's
Hate – Misery – Sorrow and Rage
They-Felt this As a Blessing
Giving to Me – What-I-Wanted from Them

(Chorus)
Death – My Death Is Drawing Near
I Lived My Life To Its Fullest
Now I'm Ready To See What Happens
Is There An Afterlife Or Nothing
If There Is – Will I Be Punished
For Being The One That Ended The World

Life is Starting to Wind-Down
I'm-Getting so Very-Very-Old
My-Queens – Doing the Same
Reports kept Coming in From the News
So-Many – Still-Dying
There is No-One left Young
Enough to Do the Hard-Work-Anymore

Leaving so Much – Untouched for So-Long
Cities-Burned to Ash – Due to Storms and Fires
It's so Weird – Watching as Mother-Earth
Kicks-Herself into Overdrive
Making-Many – New-Species of Animals
Filling-Herself-Up with New-Plant-Life
Ready to Let-Our – Carcasses be Eaten
Our-Bones – To be Covered -Up by Nature

(Chorus)
Death – My Death Is Drawing Near
I Lived My Life To Its Fullest
Now I'm Ready To See What Happens
Is There An Afterlife Or Nothing
If There Is – Will I Be Punished
For Being The One That Ended The World

There is Only a Few – Here and There
On this Planet that Mankind – Ruled for So-Long
Most of My-Queens have Already-Died
Rest are Too-Damn-Old and Sick
For-Me to Give a Damn about Anymore

I-Walk-Away to be Alone
Thinking-Back – About-My-Life
I'm-Proud of It – But it Sucks
I-Had to Be the One – The-One
Who-Brought-Forth – Doom and Gloom
I-Feel-It – My-Dying-Time is Here
Looking-Up at the Sky – Loving-It
It's so Very-Blue – Today
With a Warm – Bright – Yellow Sun
That-Puts a Smile on My-Face

World is so Beautiful
Looking at the Water and the Trees
Sitting-Down on My-Beach
Laughing – Out – Loud
I-Lay-Back to Stare – Into the Sun
In-Great-Pain and Sorrow – I-Die
Taking with Me the Rest of
All the Men and Women
Who-Call-Mother-Earth – Their-Home

(Chorus)
Death – My Death Is Drawing Near
I Lived My Life To Its Fullest
Now I'm Ready To See What Happens
Is There An Afterlife Or Nothing
If There Is – Will I Be Punished
For Being The One That Ended The World

I'm Living Death To The World
My Birth Is The Bomb
My Life Is The Fuse
My Death Will Be The Spark

I Was Born For Greatness
Destiny And Fate Had A Plan
They Got Together And Made My Birth
One For Only The Stars To Know
Putting Me Above Everyone Else

My Life Is So Great And Grand
I'm Always Right
Never Am I Wrong
I've Grabbed A Hold Of Life
Taken What I Wanted From It
Never Feeling Regret For What I Did

Death – My Death Is Drawing Near
I Lived My Life To Its Fullest
Now I'm Ready To See What Happens
Is There An Afterlife Or Nothing
If There Is – Will I Be Punished
For Being The One That Ended The World

I'm Living Death To The World
My Birth Is The Bomb
My Life Is The Fuse
My Death Will Be The Spark

(Double The Aliens = Double The Trouble: 99-100)

99. Crash Landed On Their Planet

They-Come-Out at Night
To-Feed on Humans
That-Do-Not – See-Them-Attack
In a Few-Moments
These – Invisible – Creatures
Can-Consume a Human to Their-Bones

There are Two-Different
Types of Feeding-Fanatics
There's the Meat and Blood
Chew it Up – Drink it Down
The-Other – More of A
Hideous – Creature of Foulness

These-Creatures – Eat-Up
All the Left-Over – Bones
With-Long – Clawed-Hands
They-Scoop – Them-Up
Hold-Them-Firm and Still
Eating – These – Bones
Like-They're – Carrot-Sticks

(Chorus)
Humanity Received A Big
Heart Ripping Out – When
Giant Invisible Creatures
With Empty Alien Bellies
That Have Extra Long
Sharp – Shredding Teeth
Crash Landed On Their Planet

Humanity doesn't Stand a Chance
In-Hell to Survive this Onslaught
These-Creatures are Giants
Thirteen-Feet-Tall
Alien – Looking – Monsters
Whom-Invisably – Walk-Up to a Human
And – Eats-Off of Them – A
Arm – Leg or Head

48

(Chorus)
Humanity Received A Big
Heart Ripping Out – When
Giant Invisible Creatures
With Empty Alien Bellies
That Have Extra Long
Sharp – Shredding Teeth
Crash Landed On Their Planet

Gotten so Bad at Night
That the Humans – Stay-Inside
Next-Night – After an Attack
For-Fear of Being – Eaten-Alive
Has made Governments
Lose-Sight of Objectiveness

Bullets are Shot at the Night
Never-Hitting-One of the Unseen
Who-Stands – Behind the Shooters
Waiting for Them to Stop-Shooting
After they're Relaxed and Calm
After their Weapons are Down
The-Human-Eating – Invisible-Alien
Monster-Looking-Creatures – Feast
Like-They are at a Human-Buffet

(Chorus)
Humanity Received A Big
Heart Ripping Out – When
Giant Invisible Creatures
With Empty Alien Bellies
That Have Extra Long
Sharp – Shredding Teeth
Crash Landed On Their Planet

Our-Oath of Noninterference
Is a Poke in Our-Guts
We-Want to Help – These-Humans
To do This – We-Would
Destroy – Their-Beliefs
In-Their-Way of Life

These-Misguided – Humans-Believe
What is Eating-Them – Every-Night
Are-Demons from Hell
Sent by Someone – Named-Satan
Who is the Lord of His-Hell
Because – He-Wants to Own their Souls

(Chorus)
Humanity Received A Big
Heart Ripping Out – When
Giant Invisible Creatures
With Empty Alien Bellies
That Have Extra Long
Sharp – Shredding Teeth
Crash Landed On Their Planet

Heaven and Hell
A-Fantastic – Magical-Story
That is Too-Much – Believed-In
For these Way-Too – Confused-Humans
To-Stop and Take an Objective
Look at What is Really-There

Contemplating – Loop-Holes
The-Elders – Are at a Loss
There is No-Way – We can Help
Our-Laws to Their – Very-Meaning
Tell-Us – We-Would-Do
More-Harm than Good for Mankind
With-Tears in Our-Eyes
We-Can-Not – Watch-Anymore
We-Begin – Our-Journey – Away from Earth

(Chorus)
Humanity Received A Big
Heart Ripping Out – When
Giant Invisible Creatures
With Empty Alien Bellies
That Have Extra Long
Sharp – Shredding Teeth
Crash Landed On Their Planet

(The Words Come to Us) Help-Us – Save-Us

50

To-All-Out-There – That-Can-Hear-Us
We-Need-Your-Help – We're-Under-Attack
From-Alien-Creatures that are Invisible
Their-Eating-Us by the Thousands – Every-Night
Our-Weapons are Useless for They-Leave – No-Signature
We-Have-Gold – Diamonds – Water – Food – Women
To-Pay-You for Your-Payment – Please-Help-Us!

With hundreds of small ships
We fly down to save the day
The bright sun light shines down upon us
As we come walking out of our ships
The humans fear us at first sight
This we take no offense to we're different
We're wined and dined like royalty
As we tell the humans all about
What is eating them at night
Disagreements meet us strong at first
But in a little time we're almost believed

When the night falls we're ready to attack
With humans in our ships we show them
On our screens what stalks the night
The human eyes are full of fear and rage
As we squeeze our triggers firing away
We shred these human eating monsters
Into nothing but blood spots and chunks
In a few days' time the nights on earth
Turn from killing all invisible creatures
To let's enjoy our peace of mind
Now that all the monsters are dead
We wave our hands to our victory for the humans
Then it dawns on us that humanity changes fast
When we're attacked by many armies from earth

(Chorus)
Humanity Received A Big
Kick Up Their Asses – When
Giant Invisible Creatures
With Empty Alien Bellies
That Have Extra Long
Sharp – Shredding Teeth
Crash Landed On Their Planet

51

100. Humans In Space

"Human Logic = Disaster
When Off Planet Technology
Falls Into Humanities Hands
Humans In Space = Trouble In Space
For All Those That Happily
Live Amongst The Stars"
(05-23-2014)

(The Cross Planetary Singing News Channel)
Advanced-Aliens – Crash-Landed on Earth
Started-Eating the Humans all Up
With-Help from The-Helpers
All-Eating-Aliens were Killed
Then-Not-Out of Kindness
These-Humans – Took-Over
When the Helpers had Their
Hands-Out in Friendship
The-Humans – Attacked and
Killed-Most of the Helpers

Hours-Turned to Days of Torment
For the Surviving-Helpers
As-Humans – Squeezed-All
The-Information – They-Need to Know
Out of the Helpers – With-Help
From-Lots and Lots of Pain

Satisfied the Humans got Together
Started their Own – Space-Charter
Where-Opportunity and Prosperity-Awaits
All it Takes is Human-Pride and Spirit
And the Will – Inside-You to Kill – Every
Space-Alien – That-Gets in the Way

(Chorus #1)
Hello To All Alien Worlds
Eat Your Last Meal
Make Love – Have Sex
Because Very Soon
Coming Directly To You Are
Some Pissed Off Humans In Space
From A Blue Planet Named Earth
52

(The Humans)
Eaten-Alive for Food
Was-Our-Fate – One-Day
Out of Nowhere – They-Struck
First-Night – Stained in Blood
We-Humans – Were-Prey
To so Many – Invisible-Predators

Eating-Monsters were Controlled
By-Friendlier – Looking-Aliens
That-Wanted – Nothing in Return
But to Help-Out – Us-Lucky-Humans
By-Killing – These-Creatures for Us
They-Thought – Us-Simple
They-Thought – We-Would-Not – Understand

We-Let-These – Aliens-Help-Us
We-Watched and Learned from Them
After-All-Their – Blood-Thirsty
Pets – Were-Killed-Off
We-Took-Opportunity and Triumphed
Over-Our – Would-Soon to Be
Helpful-Conquerors and Rulers

Being as Humane as Can-Be
We-Took – Our-Time-Talking
With-Our – Nicely-Kept-Guests
Keeping-Their – Safety and Needs
In-Our-Minds – While-Receiving – Our-Answers
Our-Dreams of Changing the Past
From-War – Declared on Us – to A
Friendship with These-Aliens
Was-Shattered – When-They told Us
That-Humanity is Nothing but Pet-Food
To-All the Alien-Planets in the Galaxy

(Chorus #2)
Hello To All Alien Worlds
We Are Not Your Pet's Food
We Do Not Want War – It's Your Choice
So Peace To You – From The
Humans In Space – That Want Only Peace
Please Agree – Or – We Will Have To Kill You

(The Cross Planetary Singing News Channel)
Humans – Waving-White-Flags
Have-Destroyed – Ten-Planets so Far
On their Journey – Across our Universe
They-Fire-Missiles on First-Contact
Landing after Their-Slaughter
Taking-All the Treasures of that World

Witnesses have Told of Tales
That after Battle and Wars
The-Humans – Gather-Together
Putting – Two-Fingers on Each-Hand
In the Air and Shouting-Victory

Many-Attempts have Failed to Have
Peaceful-Talks with the Humans
They will Not-Listen to Reason
While-Broadcasting – Messages-Stating
It is Not – Our-Fault
We-Humans are Not – Pet-Food
Comply to Our-Terms or
It-Will be You – Alien's-Fault
We have to Kill – All of You

Peace – We – All – Love
And Cherish in Our-Lives
Is-Over for Right-Now
We have No-Choice but to Attack
These-Humans in Space
We'll-Destroy-Them or Send-Them
Crawling-Back to Their-Earth
Enlist-Now to Save-More of Our-Lives
Destroy as Many-Humans as You-Can

(Chorus #1)
Hello To All Alien Worlds
Eat Your Last Meal
Make Love – Have Sex
Because Very Soon
Coming Directly To You Are
Some Pissed Off Humans In Space
From A Blue Planet Named Earth

(The Humans)
Space is so Cold
Space is so Lonely
This-War that the Galaxy-Started
Is a Living-Hell for Us-Humans
We-Tried – Our-Best – But
Every-Time it's the Same
Another-Alien-Planet – Attacked-Us
We-Defended-Ourselves then Attacked-Back
Destroying-Yet-Another – Non-Complying-Planet

Stop the War – We-Pray to God
But it Never-Does any Good
Has to Be – Because all These-Aliens
Don't have Any-Gods to Believe-In
We-Try to Bring-Them – Ours
All-We-Get is Resentment
From these Hateful – Godless-Aliens
We-Humans in Space – Can't-Keep-This
Going-On and On – We've had Enough
Time to Bring – Some of Earth's – Big
Weaponry to These-Human – Killing-Aliens
Human-Compassion is Dead in Us
Due to All the Loss of Human-Life

We-Attack-Planets with Our
Missiles of Mass-Destruction
One-After the Other – We-Destroy
Alien-Planet after Alien-Planet
Until there is Only a Few-Left
The-War is Almost-Over – We'll-Try
One-More-Time for Peace – It is Still
Not-Our-Fault if these Human-Eating-Aliens
Would have been Vegetarians – We-Wouldn't
Have-Had to Destroy – Almost all Alien-Life in the Galaxy

(Chorus #2)
Hello To All Alien Worlds
We Are Not Your Pet's Food
We Do Not Want War – It's Your Choice
So Peace To You – From The
Humans In Space – That Want Only Peace
Please Agree – Or – We Will Have To Kill You

(Bonus Song)

The Big Bang (266.)

Future-Mother-Earth was a Dead-Planet
Doing-Nothing-Else but That
She had Almost – All that She-Needed
Deep-Inside – Her-Frozen-Core
With-No-Way to Ignite – Her-Fire

Just like All – Living-Planets
In-All of the Galaxies – Everywhere
Life of One-Planet – Can-Only-Be
Created by the Ending-Life of Another
That-Explodes and Flies-Off into Pieces
Roaming – 'Til it Finds – What it Needs
A-Dead-Planet – That it can Insert-Itself
Into and Cause an Explosion of Life

(Chorus)
The Big Bang Ended Our Peace
With A Collision So Intense
That It Burned Our Beings To Death
Making Us Become Something Different
Beings That Have A Need For Feeding

We-Are from Billions of Years-Ago
We-Lived on this Planet
When it Was – Nothing but Dead
Life for Us – Was so Different
Different-Life-Forms – Were-We
Alive – But-Not in the True-Sense

We had No – Mortal-Shells
That-Tied-Us to the World
We-Lived – Separately from It
We-Knew – Nothing of Hunger
We-Knew – Nothing of Death
We just Lived – Our-Lives-Free

(Chorus)
The Big Bang Ended Our Peace
With A Collision So Intense
That It Burned Our Beings To Death
Making Us Become Something Different
Beings That Have A Need For Feeding

It-Took so Long for Mankind to Arrive
First-We-Lived – Off the Ash from Fire
Years-Later – We-Lived off First-Life
Then the First – Big-Change-Came

When-Life – Came-Out of the Water
We-No-Longer – Had to Feed on Scraps
We-Now-Had a Place to Live-Finally
We-Entered-These – First-Walking-Beings
Feeding-Off-Them – From the Inside

(Chorus)
The Big Bang Ended Our Peace
With A Collision So Intense
That It Burned Our Beings To Death
Making Us Become Something Different
Beings That Have A Need For Feeding

Earth went Through – Many-Changes
Even-Almost-Ending a Few-Times
We stayed Strong – Knowing that in Many-Years
There-Would be What is Called-Humans
For-Us to Feed-Off – For there Will be So-Many

Humans-Became the Perfect-Host to Feed-Off
Strong-Enough to Take – Us-Entering-Them
Able to Live-Inside-Them – 'Til-Their-Deaths
Then-We-Seep-Out and Find-Another to Live-In
For-We – Were here First and We will Survive
And – Out-Live any Life-Form that is Created

(Chorus)
The Big Bang Ended Our Peace
With A Collision So Intense
That It Burned Our Beings To Death
Making Us Become Something Different
Beings That Have A Need For Feeding

57

(Bonus Song)

Still Caught In A Dream (413.)

I-Look into the Mirror
It's-Me-Again
What-I-Remember
Doesn't-Belong to Me
I-Hate-This – I-Wish-They
Would just Leave – Me-Alone
So-I – Can-Sleep in Peace
But-Every-Time – I-Close-My-Eyes

(Chorus)
I Wake Up In The
Middle Of The Night
Still Caught In A Dream
That I Can't Slip Out Of
Making Me Feel Like
I'm Slipping Into Insanity
Because The Dream I Had
Was Not Mine Once Again

Pounding of My-Heart
Sounds like Thunder
My-Mind – Starts to Clear
As-I-Realized it Happened again
I was Forced to Find-Out
About-Someone's – Twisted-Life
As-I – Nightmared about It
They-Won't – Leave-Me-Alone
And it's Starting to Affect-Me

(Chorus)
I Wake Up In The
Middle Of The Night
Still Caught In A Dream
That I Can't Slip Out Of
Making Me Feel Like
I'm Slipping Into Insanity
Because The Dream I Had
Was Not Mine Once Again

Drinking – Does-No-Good
It only Makes it Harder on Me
To-Slip-Out of My-Nightmare
So-Every-Night – I-Pray
And-Every-Night – I'm-Ignored
I've had Enough of this Hell
Time – I-Changed – My-Dreams
So-They are Mine – Once-Again

Not – Somebody – Else's
That is Calling – Out for Me
To-Help-Them – Escape-Theirs
By-Having-Me – Siphon their Mind
So-They – Can-Have – Pleasant-Dreams
From-Now on When they Sleep
While-I only Slumber in Nightmare-Land

No – No-More of This
Not-Only – Will-I-Free – My-Dreams
From – Others' – Nightmares
I will Now – Change-My-Siphon
Still-Using-It – While-They-Sleep
But-When – I'm-Fully-Awake
To take Away – All their Dirty
Little-Secrets – That they Hide
So-Well – Away-From the World

(Chorus)
I Wake Up In The
Middle Of The Night
Still Caught In A Dream
That I Can't Slip Out Of
Making Me Feel Like
I'm Slipping Into Insanity
Because The Dream I Had
Was Not Mine Once Again

Un-Pleasant-Dreams – To-You
Bad – Bad – Dreamers
Try to Enjoy – Yourselves
As-I – Who is a We
Keeps on Every-Night
Siphoning – Your – Minds

(Never Have Sex With A Demon Trilogy: 863-865)
(Written on 12/31/2015)

Demon Slayer (863.)

God-Created-Heaven – It's-Very-Nice
God-Created Hell – It's a Stinking-Pit
Souls-Rise or Souls-Fall – Not-My
Department and I-Could – Care-Less

What-I-Care-About is Demons
Stupid and Evil – I-Hate-Them
God-Says – Let-Them-Be
If-They-Don't – Break the Rules
I-Say – No-Way – Not-Today
I-Rather-Slay – Them-All-Dead

(Chorus)
Battle Me Demon From Hell
I Am The Demon Slayer
I Slay Demons Everyday
Who Knows Demon From Hell
Maybe I've Slayed Someone You Know

Demon from Hell – Weak-Nothing
What Are-You-Going to Do – About-It
I-Tell-You – What-You-Can-Do – Demon
Shut-Up – Hold-Still – So-I-Can
Slay-You and Turn-You into Hell-Dust

Roar out Your-Evilness – Demon
Attack-Me – With the Power from Hell
Fly to the Demon-Slayer – Take-Your-Chance
Watch-Very-Closely or You'll-Miss
When I-Slay-You by Taking-Off – Your-Head
I'd-Better-Wash-Up – Before-I – Flying-Back to Heaven

(Chorus)
Battle Me Demon From Hell
I Am The Demon Slayer
I Slay Demons Everyday
Who Knows Demon From Hell
Maybe I've Slayed Someone You Know
60

Demon Lover (864.)

Demon's-Blood on My-Sword
Demon's-Blood on My-Wings
I'm-Wiping and Shaking it All-Away
When-She goes Flying-By

She's a Demon from Hell
I-Fly to Slay-Her – She-Stops
I-Cannot-Believe – My-Eyes
Her-Face is Like – An-Angel's
With a Body that Belongs in Heaven

(Chorus)
Damn Me I Love My Demon Lover
She Looks Like Heaven
Even With Her Forked Tongue
Licking Demon's Blood Off My Wings
Damn Me I Love My Demon Lover
I Would Trade My Grace Away
If She Could Be Mine Forever

I-Am the Demon-Slayer
I-Slay-Demons – Almost-Everyday
I-Try-My-Best – I'm so Drained
My-Demon-Lover – Keeps-Me-Busy
Having-Sex – I've-Grown to Lax

Turned-My-Back – Once too Many-Times
My-Demon-Lover the Perfect-Assassin
Such a Fool-I-Am – Demon-Slayer – No-More
My-Demon-Lover – Laughs so Loudly as My
Wings – Head and Body – Turns into Heaven-Dust
Remember-My-Story – Never-Have-Sex – With a Demon

(Chorus)
Damn Me I Love My Demon Lover
She Looks Like Heaven
Even With Her Forked Tongue
Licking Demon's Blood Off My Wings
Damn Me I Love My Demon Lover
I Would Trade My Grace Away
If She Could Be Mine Forever

Give Me Another Chance God / I'm A Demon Now (865.)

Give Me Another Chance God

Please-Forgive-Me – God – I-Messed-Up
Should have Slain that Pretty-Demon
Instead of Playing the Fool in Lust

Please-Forgive-Me – God – I-Messed-Up
Should-Have – Kept-On – Slaying-Demons
And – Being-Satisfied with Pretty-Angels

(Chorus)
Give Me Another Chance God
I'm Too Great Of An Angel To Stay Dead
Give Me Another Chance God
I Won't Have Sex With A Demon Again
Give Me Another Chance God
You Know You Miss Me In Heaven

I'm A Demon Now

I-Am only Thoughts
I-Feel the Hand of God
I-am-Being – Re-Created
Sex with Only-Angels this Time

Wait a Minute – Where's-My-Halo
Why-Do-I-Have Horns and A-Tail
Damn it to Hell – This is Not-Fair
I-Was the Best-Damn-Angel
What-Am-I – To-Do-Now – Slay-Myself

(Chorus)
I'm A Demon Now
How Could God Do This To Me
I'm A Demon Now
I Guess I Better Get Use To It
I'm A Demon Now
No Heaven – Hell Is Now My Home
I'm A Demon Now
I Think I Might Try To – Slain Satan

Discography (Pages 63-65)

Books 1 Through 5 Song Listing

B # = Last Number of a Book

Book One: **Who Am I?** – 1-20

Book Two: **Mind Rockin'** – 21-40

Book Three: **Big Time Love** – 41-60

Book Four: **Love High** – 61-80

Book Five: **Siphon Your Minds** – 81-100

(Example) **01.** = Original Numbering - **07.** = Book Numbering

01. I Must Go Away - 07. - Book 1
02. A Race Called Man - 03. - Book 1
03. Across The Sky (Edited Version) - 17. - Book 1
05. Justice (Edited Version) - 34. - Book 2
07. Bleeding My Beast Blood Upon the Floor - **20.** - Book 1
08. I Am Wolf - 18. - Book 1
23. Empty Hands (Edited Version) - 36. - Book 2
26. Me Myself & I - 13. - Book 1
33. Enjoy (The Eye) - 90. - Book 5
38. Darken Our Love (Edited Version) - 27. - Book 2
40. Our Love - 45. - Book 3
41. All I Need - 06. - Book 1
43. Love, Baby Love - 63 - Book 4
45. Cursed Years - 04. - Book 1
47. I'm Dying And It's Raining - 14. - Book 1
49. Rip You Apart While Drinking You Down - 19. - Book 1

54. Speak As One - 16. - Book 1
55. Push Me Away - 44. - Book 3
59. We The People - 15. - Book 1
61. Bam Burn Dead Hell (Edited Version) - 38. - Book 2
64. We Are Here - 31. - Book 2
65. The Church of No God (Edited Version) - 32. - Book 2
66. Sweet Sweet Love - 68. - Book 4
67. Who Am I? - 01. - Book 1
70. Shout (Your Day Will Come) - 02. - Book 1
72. Thickness of Mind - 22. - Book 2
73. Rock And Roll House - 10. - Book 1
74. Hero - 12. - Book 1
75. I'll Be Your Hero - 11. - Book 1
76. Tapped (Edited Version) - 30. - Book 2
77. Why - 05. - Book 1
78. Love Den (Not A Sin) (Single Version) - 08. - Book 1
79. Angel Eyes (Single Version) - 09. - Book 1

80. I Am Dream / Prelude To The Eye - 91. - Book 5
81. Stranger Calling No One - 23. - Book 2
83. Set Loose on Hell (S.L.O.H. #1) - **40.** - Book 2
84. Freaking Zombies Man - 39. - Book 2
86. Through the Flame of a Candle - 29. - Book 2
87. I love You - 26. - Book 2
96. Break Me When You're Done - 28. - Book 2
97. She Let Me Pick Her - 72. - Book 4
98. The Last Rocker - 24. - Book 2

100. Purgatory (20 Steps) (The Single) **(Purgatory's Full: No Book #)**
105. Dying While Texting - 25. - Book 2
111. 3 Can Corn Man - 35. - Book 2
113. Evil Pill - 37. - Book 2
122. Mind Rockin' - 21. - Book 2
126. Pets and Monsters - 33. - Book 2
127. You Are My Everything - 46. - Book 3
132. She's Got To Be Mine - 62. - Book 4
142. Beautiful - 54. - Book 3
156. I Can Smell Your Death - 94. - Book 5
157. I Can Sense Your Death - 95. - Book 5
166. Brave Face - 93. - Book 5
182. Protector - 86. - Book 5
199. Love - 52. - Book 3

207. Pillow Talk - 69. - Book 4
208. Birth - 96. - Book 5
209. Life - 97. - Book 5
210. Death - 98. - Book 5
217. Catch My Heart - 48. - Book 3
238. Time - 64. - Book 4
239. Stay - 65. - Book 4
240. Dressed Up Like A Diner - 83. - Book 5
249. Long Love Train Ride - 84. - Book 5
250. One Day (The Hard/We Can Do It/Our Time Is Here) - 57. - Book 3
253. The Lovers Of Forever - **60.** - Book 3
260. Peace Freaks (Gift #4 No Book #) - Book 1
261. Ordinary - 50. - Book 3
266. The Big Bang **(Bonus S. No Book #)** - Book 5
287. Power To The Mammals Who Don't Walk On Two Legs - 85. - Book 5

300. Siphon - 81. - Book 5
313. Coma Made For Me - 82. - Book 5

319. Let's Be Friends (That Sleep Together) - 76. - Book 4
320. Forget About Our Love - 77. - Book 4
323. Little By Little (Duet) - 43. - Book 3
327. High With Me - 66. - Book 4
341. Fall In Love With Me - 56. - Book 3
346. Lady From Space (Love Version) - **80.** - Book 4
361. It's So Nice To Be Loved - 42. - Book 3
381. Somebody Loves Me - 47. - Book 3
382. Big Time Love - 41. - Book 3
394. Wrap My Love All Around You - 58. - Book 3

413. Still Caught In A Dream **(Bonus S. No Book #)** - Book 5
421. Afraid Of Love - 51. - Book 3
420. A Beautiful Woman - 55. - Book 3
422. Happy Birthday Baby - 71. - Book 4
451. It's Time For Love - 75. - Book 4
456.0 Charity Is More Than A Word (Gift #3 No Book #) - Book 1
457. (I'm Busted) For I've Fallen In Love With You - 67. - Book 4
489. Take My Hand - 49. - Book 3
493. I Want To Be With You **(Bonus S. No Book #)** - Books 3 & 4
496. The Entity Of Light - 87. - Book 5
497. Lovely Heaven And Hated Hell - 88. - Book 5
498. The Entity Of Darkness - 89. - Book 5 9
499. Earth Like Planets Everywhere - 90. - Book 5

502. Makes Me Smile - 74. - Book 4
508. The Time Is Now **(Bonus S. No Book #)** - Books 3 & 4
522. Turn Me On Baby - 78. - Book 4
533. When Death Rules the World (Gift #1 No Book #) - Book 2
536. Love High - 61. - Book 4
540. Summer Time And Love - 70. - Book 4
558. She Still Has That Body - 79. - Book 4
561. Love Comes Back Around - 59. - Book 3
563. If You Need Me - 53. - Book 3
567. Peace and Death (Gift #2 No Book #) - Book 2
578. Smile If You Love Me - 73. - Book 4
583. Crash Landed On Their Planet - 99. - Book 5
584. Humans In Space - **100.** - Book 5

863. Demon Slayer **(Bonus S. No Book #)** - Book 5
864. Demon Lover **(Bonus S. No Book #)** - Book 5
865. Give Me Another Chance God / I'm A Demon Now
     (Bonus S. No Book #) - Book 5
906. I Remember Rock And Roll **(Bonus S. No Book #)** - Book 1

Hello Mind Rockers and welcome back for my rewind book, Book Five: Siphon Your Minds. Things are running their course, I am very happy about my last book that came out September 18 titled Book Six: Do You Remember Rock And Roll & Book Seven: Rock And Roll Bachelor my second 2 in 1 theme book, the twin book of Book Three: Big Time Love & Book Four: Love High. The reason why this book is coming out after Book Six & Book Seven is because I wanted to include the short story that you will be reading right after this editorial piece, titled The Vegetarian And The Slaughterhouse. For awhile I was trying to come up with an idea to add a short story to this book and also to Book Eight: The End. My wife and I were driving back home and then just like that out of the blue the title The Vegetarian And The Slaughterhouse came to me. I pondered for a moment, then the idea came to me about what would happen if a vegetarian had a slaughterhouse willed to them by the owner of the slaughterhouse. My original idea is different than the story that is written in this book.

When I started writing this story I wanted it to be non-supernatural but after I started writing it supernatural thoughts took over my mind and I let it happen. I am glad that I did because in Book Eight:The End, the short story that will be included is titled An Ordinary Day In Hell, this story is a prelude to The Vegetarian And The Slaughterhouse. The story An Ordinary Day In Hell is finished, along with the rest of Book Eight, all I have to do is go back and do some final editing and then send it to copyright, then I will release Book Eight for sale in November. So three months in a row, three new books. I am very happy that I wrote these two short stories, they really helped clear my mind so I could start over again re-writing the continuing story of Purgatory's Full – titled Set Loose On Hell. I'm very excited about where I am at in this story so much that I deleted everything that I wrote before for Set Loose On Hell. I liked what I had written before but it just wasn't clicking for me. My mind was just not in the right frame for what needed to be done for the character Kayden Hart. I've already written three new songs for Set Loose On Hell, I came up with a back story for Kayden's birth mother and his mysterious birth father. I've also came up with some ideas to bring back some characters from Purgatory's Full that now reside within Hell. I am also adding a time line to Set Loose on Hell just like there is in Purgatory's Full. Set Loose on Hell is a journey for Kayden Hart on his quest to seek out and find Satan so they can have their battle to the death. At the end of Purgatory's Full Kayden is full of love with just a few specks of unknown evil within him so his journey has to be painful, remember-able and make him worthy to face his ultimate challenge.

I cannot wait to find out what my mind will come up with for Set Loose On Hell. Thoughts have been flowing very, very nicely so much so that I have already at this point in time come up with an idea for another story, a final story for Kayden Hart that will take place after Set Loose On Hell. So once again, these books are now going to be a trilogy of stories instead of a double feature but Purgatory's Full will now be the first story instead of the middle story.

Thank you my fans once again for joining me, I'm looking forward to getting back together with you in Book Eight: The End. So until then, Peace to all of you. I hope you enjoyed the Siphoning of your minds. Mind Rock on, The Gemini Rising Rockin' Machine.

Here is the answer to how I came up with my author's name.
Gemini -
Because I am One and for its Meaning of Two
which I Use as my Muse while Writing.
Rising -
To Constantly use so I never Stop trying to
Ascend to Be and do Better.
Rockin' -
Is what I like to Do and What this is all About.
Machine -
Is a Reminder for Myself to keep Going on

(05-19-2016) I am writing to you the morning of the day that I am going to take the original version of this book off of sale and replace it with this new cover vesion with some extra added to it. I remember when the idea came to me for the lyrical story "Siphon" the chorus stayed in my mind for sevaral days later. This book, Book Five: Siphon Your Minds original number was suppose to be Book Seven: but I changed my mind so there would be a book in between this book and Book Eight: Then of course I wrote Veg/Slaughter which made this book become my first and last ever rewind book. Book Five, this book is one of my favorites for it is filled with mostly mental fantasy lyrical stories and a very great pairing to Book Eight: The End, which is mostly horror lyrical stories. I had a great time going over this book one last time, giving it a final tuning, so to say. I will being doing the same thing for Book Eight, and all my other books that I will be adding new covers to. A nice trip down memory lane I'll be taking for the next month or so. I hope you enjoyed this new and last version of Book Five. Peace to you Mind Rockers, The Gemini One.

The Vegetarian And The Slaughterhouse

The Vegetarian And The Slaughterhouse (Pages 68-86)

Stan (The Main Vegetarian Man) Floyd, accomplished what he has been trying to do for so long. His dream has come true, years and years of fighting this and now the war is over, the Slaughterhouse is officially closed. Days later, after the partying buzz has left Stan's brain, there is a knock at his door. Stan opens the door to a man standing there with a letter addressed to Stan that he has to sign for. The letter is from a lawyer firm that Stan has never had any dealings with before. Stan is thinking to himself, what this can be all about, while he is opening the letter. The letter is very short and very officially written, Stan is to come to this lawyer's firm in two days for a reading of a will, the will of the man that Stan hated so very much, the now deceased owner of the Slaughterhouse. Stan says out loud, " **** that! – No ****ing way", then throws the letter on top of the stand that he has placed beside his door.

Beet soup is on the menu, it looks so red, it looks like blood-soup. Stan's mind is on the thought of blood boiling in his pot, when he decides for himself to smell blood boiling, making him sick. Beet soup down the drain, tomato and lettuce sandwiches eaten. Stan liked the crispiness and dampness of his sandwiches, he ate three. The mirror that hangs in Stan's bathroom is full of truth, it never lies, this day, this mirror has a shard up its ass. So in reply to Stan's question there is only one word over and over screaming at his face. That word is – Coward. – The rage inside Stan is Rising. That rage the one that Stan Created – The one he Wanted – The one he Needs, is bubbling up into a song that Stan can sing out loud – with Pride.

I Slaughter – The Slaughterhouse
The Old Damn Bastard – Is Dead
He Died While Killing Animals
One Moment With Blood On His Hands
He Grabbed His Chest – Then He Died – Then I Won The War
No More Blood! – No More Blood!
The Slaughterhouse Is Closed Forever
If The Old Damn Bastard Wants Forgiveness
He Can Kiss My Alive Ass – To Death
I Hate Him & I'm Glad – That He Is Dead
I Hope He Is Burning In Hell
I Hope He Feels Like One Of The Animals He Killed
I Slaughter – The Slaughterhouse (13)

(Two Days Later)

Stan (The Main Vegetarian Man) Floyd, shows up late and right on time, his time. Stan (The Main Vegetarian Man) Floyd, is going to own this place when he walks in the door. Stan walks into a barely lit reception room, looks around at the no bodies around and ponders. Down the hall there is a light, one office lit up all nice and not friendly. Walking to this lit office is taking a very long time, Stan walks faster the office seems further away, "What the ****!" Stan says out loud in fear. Stan stops walking and the office holds still like a waiting, illuminated predator. Stan walks very slowly, the office illuminates even brighter. The word Coward is what is on Stan's mind as he keeps his long, slow steady pace towards the freakish thing he has never experienced before. Nine steps more to go and the office scoots towards Stan like it's saying hurry up and enter, I dare you, you scared to Hell cowardly Coward.

The sound of Stan's heartbeat, beating out of his chest, should be enough to stop Stan from reaching for the door knob, but no, Stan has to know what lies behind this Hellish door that he fears to death. 1-2-3 turn the beeping door knob Stan – You only live once. The brightness blinds Stan upon entering this very hot office. Stan cannot believe his eyes – Stan has entered the office of Hell – Stan laughs. The bright light starts to slowly dim, there is a sound of something being placed down upon the floor, then once again, only heavier and bigger. What is this I am seeing? – This cannot be – You're Dead – You're Dead. The Old Damn Bastard is sitting in a chair, behind a desk, smiling, wearing a black suit, smoking a cigar, having the time of his death. (Silence & Staring) (Ticking of a Clock) (It is so Damn Hot)
(Shouting out in Song from the Old Dead Damn Bastard)

I Come To Eat Your Soul To Death
You Vegetarian Bastard
Then – Ha Ha
I'm Going To Make You
Eat Bloody Raw Meat
Right Off The Living Never Dying Animals
That You Will Eat Forever
While Rotting & Screaming &
Bleeding & Burning In Hell
I Am Your Hell Tormentor
Your Forever Bringer Of Pain
Get Ready To Die Bad & Burn In Hell
You Horrible Vegetarian Bastard (13)

(Stan is Scared to Death) (Stan does not want to Die)
(Stan is too Scared to Scream) (Stan cannot Move)
(Stan is too Scared to Run away from his offering from Hell)

"Just look at your face, your expression, it's priceless, just look at my eyes, I'm laughing so hard, I'm crying from making you look like a fool. You deserved that Stan, after all, you tormented me 'til my heart could not take it any more and I died from your endless torturing. Relax Stan, I had to do this to you, you deserve it and you know it. But now that is over, it is now time for you to hear your deal, take a seat Stan, get comfortable you have a big deal that you have to think very seriously about." "What is this?" Stan asks, "What do you want?" "Have a seat and I will tell you everything very, very, crystal clear Stan." (Stan nervously and slowly sits down in the single chair provided)

As soon as Stan's ass sits on the chair the door opens and in walks a wicked looking young lawyer, with a briefcase in hand, wearing a black suit and sun glasses, with a smiling I rule the world with Hell beside me, look on his face. "Hello Mr. Vegetable Head, I am Mr. Dark the attorney for Mr. Meat." "That's Mr. Long Meat, Mr. Dark – Get it Right. Extra Long – Extra Charred from the Glorious Flames of Hell." "Pardon me Mr. Vegetable Head, I am Mr. Dark the attorney for Mr. Long Meat, I am sure you remember him, after all, you with your wicked ways helped end the mortal life of my client even sooner than expected. If I could I would sue you on behalf of my client for making him die, you very evil, meat hating,Vegetarian man."

(Stan is not use to taking this kind of Crap from anybody.
Stan remembers his song, I Slaughter – The Slaughterhouse (13)
says **** it & sings it out loud to his two hosts from Hell.)

The two Hell hosts are pissed to Hell and just about ready to tear into Stan, when Stan says, "Mr. Dark huh, looks more like Mr. Dork to me. And you, you old dead bastard, you're Mr. Long Meat, like Shit you are. As in life you are in death – nothing but a Meatless old bastard that can never get it up unless you are killing innocent – defenseless animals." "You pig face Vegetarian, son of a pig face pig, I hate you, I'm going to make you burn forever starting right now," Mr. Meatless screams. "Now gentlemen calm down this is not the way this proceeding is suppose to proceed," says Mr. Dark, very composedly.

"Mr. Long Meat don't forget who sent you up here for this proceeding, believe me you don't want to go there. Satan will grab your soul and rip it apart for failing to carry out his orders to their very Hellish fullest. Apologies, Mr. Floyd, I was going for a little levity." "And very little at that Mr. Dark," Stan replies with more control in his voice. "Touche, Mr. Floyd. Let's get on with this shall we then? I represent, Mr. Wheat, the past and perhaps future owner of Wheat's Meats and more important than that, their Slaughterhouse, the very one that you love that is closed right now. The reason you were summoned here today Mr. Floyd has to do with this very same Slaughterhouse. It is my pleasure to inform you Mr. Floyd that you are now the new owner of Wheat's Slaughterhouse. Mr. Wheat left this to you in his will. Congratulations, Mr. Floyd."

"Great, very great, Mr. Dark, I'll just keep it closed then, until forever. Don't understand all the Hellish drama and I don't care and in closing thank you Mr. Wheat you dumb ass, I guess you don't understand the concept of the meaning of paying someone back that wronged you in your past life." Mr. Wheat says, "You see this as a gift, you fool, I cursed your soul with the words I spoke out to one of Hell's secretaries, as I agreed to sell my soul to Satan for a chance to damn your soul. Even better a chance to switch my soul with yours, your soul takes my place in Hell, while my soul enters your body, so I can do a lot of Satan's work on Earth, all in your name. I will turn you into a meat eating machine, that tells all vegetarians to kiss his ass. How's my Payback now Mr. Floyd?"

Mr. Floyd says, "What kinda shit is this? How can this animal killing monster, curse my soul? I never agreed to sell my soul, my soul is mine, free and clear from all this crazy ass hell." Mr. Dark responds, "Very correct Mr. Floyd, your soul is yours, it is safe, for now. But very soon that soul that is yours will be tested, perhaps your soul is not as strong and as hard as you feel that it is. Hell is coming for your soul Mr. Floyd. Hell is the grandest show in the universe, it has been performing in front of souls just like yours, since God gave them to you. But that's the End, right now, is the beginning, your soul is safe as long as you follow the terms in Mr. Wheat's will. You are the new and only owner of the slaughterhouse, if you try to sell it or give it away or try to destroy it or even try to turn it into another business, you will be in violation of the terms of this said will."

"In truth all you have to do is live the rest of your life like you want, while owning the slaughterhouse to your dying day. If you do this, you are in the free and clear from Hell, of course your judgment could change that, but that is for even later." Mr. Floyd says, "All I have to do is own a slaughterhouse, what's so hard about that?" Mr. Wheat laughing, " I'll tell you what's hard about that, Veg head." Mr. Dark says, "Please Mr Wheat, let me be the one to continue this will's terms. The hard Mr. Floyd is what I already stated, Hell is coming for your soul. Your days, your nights, your dreams, your hopes even your love life will all have Hell's full attention. Hell will be merciless, Hell will rip at your life, scarring your soul, until it feels like it's dead and you no longer want it inside you anymore. Then on that day Mr. Floyd, Hell will gain its prize. One more thing Mr. Floyd there is an out right here and now, you can walk away from all of this and not be the owner of the slaughterhouse, but all that you did, all that you had to live with, will all be for nothing. Because if you say you want out of this, well the slaughterhouse will have one great big bloody reopening all because you were too scared to stand up to the challenge." (Silence & Thinking) Mr. Floyd says, "I Accept, Bring It On."

(One Month Later)

No snakes in the garden yet, Satan and Hell must be all talk, I shook for a week over what I got myself into. Now after a month has gone by, it feels more like an almost forgotten dream to me. Big date tomorrow night, early to work in the morning, I'm tired might as well head to bed. (Calmness of sleep turns into a Hellish nightmare for the first time for Stan, the first of many to come in the years ahead.)

(The First Hell Dream Of Many)

I'm walking in a giant garden, beautiful plants and flowers are everywhere, glowing the growing light of life. I'm at peace, I could stay in this wonderful garden forever, this is Heaven to me. Out of the corner of my eye, I see something, I turn towards it, nothing is all I see now. Why is this bothering me? There is nothing there, I'm at peace, why can't I turn away? I cannot stop staring at the nothing that was not there. I'm getting a little pissed, because my mind is telling me that in this dream I'm supposed to get laid. Finally. Damn that was weird, let it pass, time to step back inside my dream and watch myself have some fun, she is so hot. What the Hell was that? Nothing? I hate it, I don't know why but that nothing feels to me, I don't know, like it is me, a me that I don't want to be. I feel so dark, I'm angry and I hate this! I want to be turned on, in this dream I get laid, right?

I hear high heels walking towards me, I look towards the sound and there she is my dream lady, Samantha, dressed like a sexy librarian, that turns me on so much. I watch as Samantha takes off her clothes, revealing an even sexier red teddy. I have been making love to her & **** her for as long as I can remember. I love her, she has given me with her love & her body, the confidence I need to complete things in my life, like closing down that damn dead, blood thirsty, Hellish, nightmarish Slaughterhouse. She speaks to me, after we get done, I lay my head on her lap, she rubs my temples, telling me things to do with such a gentle, soft, sexy, lovely voice, I'm in dreamland inside my wanted comfortable dream. She then lovingly places her precious thoughts and wants inside my mind for my conscious mind to follow when they come to it like a gentle whisper inside my mind. I love her so much. Why does she look scared of me? Come to me my perfect dream lady, I want to feel you for as long as I can dream tonight.

I can't hear you, your voice is gone my dream lady. Come to me, I want to kiss you, I want to bite you, and I want to taste your blood. Come to me my dream lady. Tonight you will be my love slave, I'm going to give you a loving tonight like I have never given you before. Come here now! I want you, stop shaking in fear, come closer so I can take off your clothes and while you're at it, bring that rope that is lying beside your feet, I will put it to good use. What the Hell? Why am I turned on? Why am I saying these things? Why am I wanting this? With tears in her eyes, my dream lady brings me my rope and her soul to taste and enjoy to sexual death. I cannot stop myself. Okay this is enough, I'm not turned on anymore, time to change this dream, think I'll make her walk back in wearing pink this time, damn what a dream. My dream lady will not stop walking towards me, she is crying. I scream stop, stop, she will not listen to me. I don't know if she can even hear me at all. She is so scared. I cannot help her, all I can do is watch what is about to happen, without being able to do anything about it.

My dream lady is dead, she was tied up, enjoyed by the I that is not me. While lust was in full bloom, my dream lady changed into a scary looking twisted and damned version of herself. I listened to her say things that she never said before. At the end when I that is not me was finished with my dream lady, she begged and begged to be killed, and laughed out loud, so very happy when the I that is not me told her very calmly what he was going to do to her, how she was going to die. The sick Bastard took his time, I tried to turn away, but like a very bad accident, I could not help myself, I watched in horror, hating this murdering, I

I watched still not being seen, when the I that is not me looked at me and smiled then reached down and soaked his hands in the blood of my now dead dream lady. Then the I took his hands and wiped all the blood off of them all over his face. I'm scared. I laughed then pointed at me, I looked at the finger, the blood on it was dripping off landing on the floor. I cannot move I am stuck inside my dream as the I that is not me walks towards me telling me that he is going to kill me. The I that is not me is staring into my eyes, then I smacks me in my forehead really hard making a loud smack sound. Damn that hurt, piece of damn shit, hitting me in my forehead like that, I want to kick his ass but still I cannot move, I is laughing like a jackass, then like he wasn't laughing at all he stops and turns his back to me. The I that is not me starts to back up towards me when he reaches me instead of touching me he inserts himself inside me. I is gone, all that there is left, is I?

I wake up hot and sweaty, man what a ****ing dream. I look over at my alarm clock and it goes off scaring me, ha, ha, damn. Time to go to work, today is another day to stop people from killing animals. Night time, time for my date, I hate blind dates, well some times they end up alright. I'm dressed and ready to go, waiting for my blind date Samantha, to show up to pick me up, which is weirding my mind out knowing that she has the same name as my now dead dream lady. This is the first time a date picked me up, it's a little weird, like it doesn't feel quite right. Door bell, I hope she's hot and tells me after seeing me that she wants dessert first. I'm in shock as I open the door to my dream lady, Samantha, whose face I know so well, she is wearing a long jacket which suddenly opens up revealing her sexy body and the same sexy red teddy that she died wearing last night in my dream. I'm staring in silence when my date says to me I know that I am pretty but you can talk to me, I won't bite you where you don't want me to. I laugh at her joke, trying to shake this damn freakiness out of my mind.

She is so beautiful, I feel so weak, I snap out of it and invite Samantha inside. We decide not to leave, we drank two drinks and we're on my couch kissing, Samantha is letting me touch her wherever I want, so I go for it and ask if she would like to go to my bedroom so we can make love. Samantha quickly tells me yes, but first she has to go to the ladies room, she wants me to wait for her there naked. I've been naked for twenty minutes, should I? So I walk to knock on my bathroom door. Knock, knock, you ok Samantha? No answer but I hear movement then like a quiet growl, Samantha tells me that she is fine and for me to go back to my bedroom so she can rock my world. Something is not right, maybe I should get redressed but I'm so damn horny it's been a week since I've gotten laid.

I laugh at the thought, I been with weirder before so I go back inside my bedroom and stay naked. Five minutes later Samantha comes running into my bedroom like a wild woman with her face painted in her own blood. "**** me, **** me," Samantha screams then jumps on top of me while I'm sitting on my bed. I scream and push her off me. She laughs and tells me to taste her blood. I shout at Samantha, "What the ****'s wrong with you?" Samantha stops laughing, looks me right in my eyes and says, "Ok no sex well just have death then." Samantha then pulls a knife out, waves it around then before I can say anything she stabs herself over and over, right in her heart. I run towards her trying to stop her but all I can do is take the knife out of her dying hand that is covered in her blood. My blind date Samantha is dead on my floor, bleeding all over it and I have her murder weapon in my hand.

What the Hell am I going to do? No one will believe me, I can't believe I am telling myself to do this, but I don't want to go to jail for killing someone that I did not kill. A few hours later my bedroom is cleaned up, Samantha's dead body is disposed of and I am stepping out of my shower clean but not cleansed. A couple of days later the cops are knocking on my door, asking me if I have seen Samantha, that she has been missing since the day before we had our date. I calm down and tell the cops that we were suppose to have a date, a blind date and she never showed up. So I figured she lost her nerve and decided just not to show up and not worry about calling me, so I decided to just let things be and not call her back either. The cops listen to my tale, thank me for my time then they leave me alone so I can relive the death Hell dream that happened a few days ago.

(One Year After The Dream Became Real)

(Stan can see all kinds of Crazy – Evil – Shit now, it is driving him a little bit Hard, a little bit Soft. Evil is sexy and it is also damning to see happen in front of you, even if you're getting off. Stan has become an evil lady lovin' machine, just enjoying himself. Dipping his Veg-head in all that sexy evil makes Stan want it even more the next time. Yup, Stan has turned into a sex addict for hot sweet evil fine tail. Stan walks the streets during the day, walking by checking out the evil ladies that always say yes to him no matter who they belong to. Evil love has no boundaries, Satan commands every evil lady that he owns on Earth to say yes to Stan, if he asks them if they want to screw. Stan could care a Hell less about any of the Hell ladies that he screws. He hates that they control him with their evil sexy lust that is so overwhelming, that in this short of time has made Stan say **** it, what else can I do? I'm an evil lust helpless slave, but at least I'm treated like I'm the King of Sex.)

(Night Time = Total Evil – Running Free & Having Full Evil Fun)
(One year going by makes Stan a know all kinds of evil type of vegetarian guy. Day time means getting laid time with all the evil men lying dormant away from the sun of the day. Night time is something very different, evil men the killing predators of the night like to party, get laid and kill humans that ask Satan for some help. They lick their chops with a gleam shining so evil bright in their eyes waiting for the chance to make some blood flow out so they can feel it on their hands and taste it on their tongues. Evil men are not allowed to kill Stan but they are allowed to kick his ass and make him bleed a little bit. Stan learned the hard way that evil doesn't give a shit, it is the cause of almost all of the unnatural death on Earth. It is the needle in the junkie's arm, it is the bullet in a murderer's gun, the tip of the blade that is covered and dripping with such thick red human blood. Death and more death is what is served every day especially at night, humans, the weak ones have evil enticing them as they are at their lowest or at their highest. A few days after that crazy night Samantha, Stan's blind date, killed herself, Stan wanted some human contact, in other words Stan wanted and needed to get laid. What could go wrong?)

(Flash back in 1 – 2 – 3 – Now)
I'm so cold, Samantha's blood pouring out of her heart, I can't get it out of my mind. Her blood stained my hands, it was so red then in moments it turned black, like Hell dried it solid making it so hard to wash off. I had to chisel it away little bit by little bit, making a constant black blood, chunk filled stream running down my kitchen drain. Stop it. Stop it Stan, that was Hell telling you it is alive and doing fine. I must be strong, I must live my life telling Hell to kiss my Vegetarian ass. This night I walk my streets afraid inside but I don't show it because I know Hell is watching me and I'm tired of waiting at home all alone trying to stay away from it by locking myself up nice and tight, cutting all life that is outside my door away from my eyes, heart, body and soul. I've done this many times Stan says to himself as he prepares himself to walk inside his favorite bar, I need to get laid, like really bad.

(The door pulled back and the sound of Paranoid playing comes straight at Stan's ears, Stan just smiles and says out loud yes I am. The eyes of sinners look up and over at Stan's entering, the smell of alcohol, sweat, smoke and perfume hits Stan's nose like a forgotten friend that Stan has missed so much. Stan is trying to tell himself that everything is cool that everything is just fine, but as Stan's eyes look into the crowd that is drinking and trying to have sex, their eyes are telling Stan come on in and have a drink, if you dare.)

(Stan is sitting at the bar drinking his third drink, with many failed attempts at scoring for Stan to wonder just what the Hell is going on.)

I just don't get it, it's like I'm too damn ugly to get me some tonight, but that is not quite right as well because I'm getting all kinds of looks that tell me that several ladies here tonight are interested. But for some reason or another none of them are allowing the chance to happen, Stan is thinking to himself when out of nowhere a bottle is broken over his head. "What the Hell are you doing here you pretty face bastard?" Stan hears coming from the asshole that just busted the beer bottle over his head. Stan replies, "To **** your woman," right after he punched the asshole in his balls. Got to get up, got to get up, got to forget about the blood that is pouring out of my head, because this asshole is not alone. Stan looks around after he is on his feet and he is right, three more assholes are coming towards Stan to make him bleed some more. Bring it are the next words that come out of Stan's mouth as he prepares himself for some more bloody pain. Stan is lying on the floor with four assholes kicking him at their leisure when all of a sudden they stop like it is on cue and walk away laughing saying to themselves that they enjoyed themselves and they can't wait to do it again and again.

"Can I buy you a drink and wipe away the blood on your face Stan?" a very beautiful woman is asking me as my mind is starting to stop spinning around. "Sure why the hell not? And how do you know my name?" I ask. "My name is Kelly," Kelly says laughing, "Stan everyone here knows who you are. You are Satan's new whipping boy and we are his living minions that live here on Earth to do his bidding. So it is up to you Stan, more pain? Or do you want to sit down with me and have a talk while drinking a safe drink?" "Lead the way Kelly you sexy evil lady," I say, picking my bloody self up off the floor. An hour has gone by and I am feeling a lot better with three more drinks in me, the conversation Kelly and I are having has switched back and forth between us having sex with each other to what Hell has in store for me.

"Kelly right now I feel so good and Hell can kiss my ass, all I want to do is make love to your sexy evil laced body. What do you say Kelly, shall we get out of here and have ourselves some sexy fun?" "Out of here? We are going nowhere Stan, we will just have our fun right here in front of everyone," Kelly says to me with amusement in her voice. "Look Kelly I'm no prude but no way am I taking off my clothes in front of all these evil future Hell beings." With no more humor in her voice Kelly tells me, "Like you have a choice in the matter Stan, now be a good boy and take off your clothes for me."

I say to Kelly, "You're joking right?" Kelly just shakes her head no while getting up from our table, then when she is standing all the way up she throws the rest of her drink in my face. I scoot back in my chair then I try to rub Kelly's drink out of my eyes, when I pull my hand away from my eyes, Kelly's hands are just a few inches away from grabbing me around my throat. Then bam I'm grabbed by Kelly around my throat and pulled out of my chair like it is no effort at all. I cannot breathe, Kelly's grip is like a vice that I cannot pull away from, then I am thrown across the room, sailing in the air very fast and when I land the impact is so hard that I am almost knocked out. I am trying to shake away my second beat down of the night, when I feel Kelly sit herself on top of me, I look at her, she is so beautiful, then the pretty picture that is Kelly, changes right before my eyes into this ugly and stinking hag with a mouth full of extra long teeth. Kelly the hag covers my mouth telling me to shut the Hell up, then she reintroduces herself as The Hell Witch from Purgatory that now resides in Hell. I try to scream, but my mouth is covered too tightly for me to do so.

The Hell Witch then tells me it is now time for me to feel some pain that comes straight out of Hell. Moments later I cannot move because she has carved some symbols into my body. Then with chomping teeth The Hell Witch takes a big thick bite out of my chest pulling away with a big chunk of my flesh in her mouth. The pain is unbelievable but not as unbelievable as watching my flesh being eaten right in front of me like I am dinner for this bloody human meat hungry, crazy ass Hell Witch. It takes three more bites of my flesh to finally satisfy this damn Hell Witch before she stops eating me. She starts to laugh like Hell is tickling her, getting off on all the pain she has caused me to feel. I am in so much pain when The Hell Witch tells me to stay quiet, then with no mercy at all she rips away the symbols from my flesh that is keeping me paralyzed. The Hell Witch sticks her hands that are covered with my blood in my mouth making me taste my own blood. I'm spitting my own blood out when The Hell Witch comes up to me, picks me up and body slams me across a table putting me straight through it, making the table smash into pieces. "What the **** is going on?" I say out loud when The Hell Witch is standing above me and says to me, "I dare you to call me a skank, you pretty face bastard." "What?" I say. "Never mind Stan that is a different story, but what is important now Stan is that you are marked, look around and tell the difference." I look around at all the people in the bar that just watched me get my ass kicked by The Hell Witch and they have changed or in better terms the veil that was keeping the looks of Hell away from them has now been lifted.

I listen to The Hell Witch tell me that from now on, Hell will no longer be hidden from me, that I will see it and see it very clearly whenever I come across it. Then just like that the hag turns into beautiful looking Kelly once again then she disappears right in front of my eyes saying right before she is gone, "See you in Hell, Stan."

(The flashback is over and it is one year later once again.)

(This scene starts off with Stan wanting to go to his favorite bar, but is being hassled by three evil ladies that want to please him again.)
"Please, please evil ladies keep your little evil hands to yourselves, I've had all three of you more than once you should be thankful for that. Now away from me you go evil ladies I don't want or need you again." Hissing, the hottest one replies, "Stan you are so lucky that Satan wants your soul because if he did not the three of us would rip you apart you arrogant asshole." "I hate you too, you damned evil bitches, now **** off, I'm on my way to screw some evil ladies that are not you." Stan walks away from the pissed off evil ladies and continues his walk only to come across another evil lady that he has screwed before, wanting him again. Stan just laughs at her and keeps on walking by not interested.

Stan looks up ahead and standing there is Mr. Wheat and Mr. Dark waiting for him in front of his favorite bar. "Mr. Floyd are you ready to give back the slaughterhouse?" asks Mr. Dark. "Not today, I'm on my way to get laid and I don't have the time to waste talking to two ass head Hell flunkies, who don't know anything about getting laid, unless you're in the shitter whacking off on top of the shit you just shat out right before you started whacking off." "I'll wipe my ass on your face you sorry veggie bastard," Mr. Wheat screams. Mr. Dark puts up his hand in a hush gesture saying, "Mr. Floyd, I usually don't care too much about people like you, you are just another damned soul that Satan wants to get his claws on. But I got to hand it to you, you piece of shit, now you pissed me off, I'd like to rub your face on the sidewalk, but I am Mr. Cool. So instead I'll just twist the knife in a lot deeper. You're going to pay for those words you spoke to me. Of course I could just let Mr. Wheat take his shot at you, but you would just whip his ass, making a scene that Satan doesn't want to be seen."

"And Mr. Wheat back away from me some you're too damn close and your breath stinks, just because you are in Hell doesn't mean you shouldn't brush your damned teeth." "Job getting to you, Mr. Dork?" Stan asks laughing. "Don't worry about it, just go get laid and I hope she has crabs," Mr. Dark replies, sounding like the pressure from his hellish duties are getting to him.

"Sounds like you are the one that needs to get laid Mr. Dark. Why don't you come on inside and have a drink with me? I'll even let you have the evil lady that I don't pick to screw, but don't worry if she drinks enough maybe she'll let you lick her shoes," Stan says like he's about to bust a gut from trying not to laugh his ass off. "And Mr. Dork here on Earth we drink our drinks with our mouths not like you do in Hell by sucking up your Hell drinks with your nasty ass."

The two that are from Hell just look at Stan like they want to kill him, saying nothing more then right before Stan enters his favorite bar Mr. Dark says, "Here have a drink on me, Mr. Floyd," throwing a crumbled twenty dollar bill, "You're going to need it." Stan looks down at the crumbled twenty dollar bill then enters the bar leaving it where it landed for a lucky person walking by to pick it up, so happy that they found it because now today they have money to buy food instead of rummaging through garbage cans to find something spoiled to eat.

(As soon as Stan enters his favorite bar it is the same thing, different day, happening right away. Stan buys a drink, a moment later Stan is looking over at least five or six evil ladies to pick to screw today. Then like on cue, the non-evil guys that were just trying to get something going on with these evil ladies, come over all pissed off wanting their ladies back that was making it so easy on them until Stan walked in, then all the evil ladies do the same thing like they always do, turn real ugly to the guys that they were going to let have them by yelling at them to get away from them because they are so small and Stan is the Man that can please them all in the same day kind of guy.)

"Ladies, ladies, you look so fine in this dark place, now gather closely together, I want to pick the one I want first, right after I finish this drink, maybe two more after that." (Evil ladies loved to be played with, but just like real living loving ladies, if they are not picked first, then they're second best or worse and this can turn a bunch of smiling and willing evil ladies into pissed off, I'm going to rip out your eyes for being picked first really quick, type of evil ladies. While Stan is enjoying having his pre-game ritual he notices a very beautiful and very alive sex lady looking at him like he is the stud of the world and wants to find out if this is true or not for herself.)

(Lara has had enough of being a good girl, always waiting for the man that she wants to be with look at her then he waits too long and someone that she does not want to be with comes over to her, trying to do what she wanted the other man to do and then that moment is gone, for he walks away leaving her alone with another man that she does not want to be with.)

Not this time Lara says to herself, ok breathe Lara, you're hot, men love the way you look, but this time Lara you're going to get the man that you love the way he looks. Just look at all those sluts, none of them stand a chance.

"Excuse me, excuse me, that's better," Lara says when she is standing a few inches right in front of Stan. "Hush." Lara says to Stan as he is getting ready to speak to her, "I don't know who you are or if you're rich or famous, I just want your body. Now before you answer me take a very close look at me, then take an even closer look at what you would be stuck with." Lara just stands there waiting, looking so beautiful. Stan smiles so big, just loving that this has happened to him, it has been so long since he has had sex with a normal non-evil lady.

"Hello beautiful, I am Stan and you are?" "I am Lara the hottest lover in the world." "Well Lara let's start our love connection with a drink shall we?" "Most definitely Stan," Lara replies so happily. "Let's have a seat at a table," Stan suggests, "and away from all these very mad ladies." (An hour has gone by, Stan is having the best time he has had since he became the new owner of the slaughterhouse. Lara cannot believe the feelings she is having, what started as wanting to have a good time has turned into thinking that she is falling in love with Stan and she doesn't care.)

"Would you like to go to my apartment?" Lara asks. "I would love to," replies Stan so very much wanting to. (One moment there are smiles and lust wanting to be shared by two people that want and need each other, then like a super fast moving storm that moment can turn into a nightmare with the blink of an eye. Stan is staring at Lara then out of nowhere a glass is broken by one of the evil ladies that Stan passed on today against their table then that glass is slashed across Lara's throat, making Lara bleed to death in mere moments. Stan is helpless to save Lara because all the other jealous evil ladies get in his way to make sure Stan pays for his indiscretion.)

"You evil ****ing bitches why did you do that? She meant no harm to you. I just wanted one day away from all of your evil and hate. I would not have stayed with her for I would not have wanted her to share my evil burden that your master Satan dangles in my face everyday until the day I finally die and be set free from all this Hell," Stan shouts out in a rage that is so filled with evil and hate that all the evil ladies take a step back from the fear of it. I got to get out of here, her blood, her blood it is everywhere, God where the **** are you? I need your help. Where the **** are you? I need you your strength, I feel like there is no hope. I feel like my soul is dying and all you do is stay in your Heaven where there is no Hell around for you to deal with. Well God your freedom from evil is fine for you and your Heaven but it does not mean a ****ing thing to me and all the other people on your Earth that has to deal with it every single day. (Tears run down Stan's face as he runs towards the door to trying to escape his pain.)

"How was that drink, Mr. Floyd?" a laughing Mr. Dark asks. (Stan is about to go off, but is stopped by Mr. Dark before he can say a word.) "Mr. Floyd, you don't have a normal life anymore. You want sex, you got it but only with evil ladies. If you try to have sex with a normal living non-evil lady, she will be killed by one of the many evil ladies that live here on earth. You can say **** it Mr. Floyd and go for it thinking that you can hide you sex life away from Hell. You will always be mistaken and their blood will be on your hands for trying to out smart Hell. It's your choice Mr. Floyd you have free will. But if this makes you feel a little bit better and easier on you for you to make your choice, Lara was a good soul and even though her life ended very quick and very bloody, her soul is just fine, living in Heaven forevermore." (Stan has only two words for Mr. Dark.)

(Ten years have gone by, Stan's soul is dulled by evil now.)
"How can I tell Tracie that I cannot marry her ? I love her so much, I don't even know how I have kept our relationship a secret for so long from Hell. I got to find a way to get her alone tonight before it is too late. Something is just not right and I got to end this before something terrible happens to her." (Stan arrives at Tracie's family's house with his head hug down low, noticing all the cars that are parked in the driveway, around the house and down the street.) "Come on in here Stan," Tracie's father says to me after opening the door to me with a big smile on his face. "Hello William, how are you doing tonight?" I ask, walking into his home. "Fine just fine Stan. Martha and I are just so happy that you and Tracie are getting married, that we just could not wait anymore so we told the whole family and decided to throw you and Tracie this surprise engagement party."

(One hour has gone by, with lots of cheers and happiness given to the couple by the guests of the party. Stan has finally had the time and a moment alone with Tracie to talk to her, to tell her that he has something to talk to her about in private.) (Ding dong.) "I'll get it," William says to the party guests, (Bang – a gun shot fills the air like a scream.) "Get down Tracie," I tell her as I run towards the door. "Come back Stan!" Tracie screams at me in terror of the same thing happening to me. I reach the door and standing there are lots of angry evil ladies and evil men all with guns and weapons in their hands. "Stand aside," a familiar voice says out loud to the crowd of evilness. Mr. Dark walks himself in the house with that same damn smile on his face, "Mr. Floyd, Stan, all the blood that will be spilled here tonight is all your fault. I warned you but just like all like you, you think that you can fool Hell. The only fool is you. Now get out of the way and maybe you will only receive a small beating for your lingering transgressions against the force of Hell that will soon own your worthless soul."

(Stan tries to fight off the mob of evil but in mere moments he is beaten down and held in place while the evil mob enjoys themselves as they kill everyone at the party tonight. The sound of bloody mayhem turns to eerie silence as one by one the party guests fall down dead screaming and wondering why this is happening to them all. When it is finally over Stan is left alone, alive waiting on the police to come with guns ready to use on whoever were the ones to do all this murdering, but all they find is Stan crying saying to himself, no more blood.)

(A few days later Stan wakes up, takes a piss, then sits on his couch
for hours doing three things, thinking, breathing & scratching.)
(Door Bell) (No Moving) / (Door Bell) (No Moving)
(Door Bell) (Stirring) / (Door Bell) (**** Off)

"Now Mr. Floyd is that any way to talk to the man that can let you let go of all this Hellish endless pain? Does this mean you do not want to give back the slaughterhouse, Mr. Floyd?" (Foot Steps) "Come on in, Mr. Dark you little stinking prick. Where is the old dead bastard? Not that I miss his gloating, but I just don't understand it, Mr. Dark. Of all the people in Hell that Satan could have used to be the one to get a soul and return to Earth with it, Satan picks this piece of shit that is nothing but pathetic and unworthy of this high regard." Mr. Dark laughs saying, "Yeah, Satan was the one to pick Mr. Wheat alright." "What does that mean?" I ask. "That means nothing for you right now, that is a matter that directly relates to Hell, if you want that answer, give up the slaughterhouse come to my office tomorrow and then your soul can go to Hell where it belongs." Stan cannot take it anymore the Pain – the Blood – so with no more will inside him, Stan surrenders to the Old Dead Bastard the next day. Vice Versa, two souls switching reality, Stan (The Main Vegetarian Man) Floyd, is now Soulless, his Soul now belongs to Satan the Devil of Hell. The Old Dead Bastard's Soul looks like it's being put together sloppy ass like, with unequal parts of Fire – Blood & Shit, one very Ugly, Nasty – Soul ready to leave Hell, coming back to Earth to Rot and Slaughter. Hell-Soul looks at Stan and starts to Sing out loud his Song **(13)** then stops when it realizes that its song no longer applies and says **** it. Hell-Soul laughs with Hell splendor, stops suddenly, spits into Stan's damned face and says, "**** you, Veg-Head, I won, I get Earth once again, you get my Hell."

The Hell-Soul that is bound for Earth stops rising when there is a loud bang from where Veg-Head is, the Hell-Soul looks down and watches as Stan (The Main Vegetarian Man) Floyd, turns into Satan? With all of Hell's splendor, shining so Hellish burning bright. Satan smiles and snaps his fingers making the tiny damned soul of the Old Damn Bastard appear in his hand. "Welcome to Hell, Mr. Wheat. This is your introduction day, a way for me to mess with your mind before I take your worthless soul and dip it head first into a big giant pit filled with burning shit."

(Mr. Wheat is so freaked out and so very scared) "Please Satan, don't do this to me, I can be your man on Earth, I will do whatever you want. Please Satan, let me have this chance at life once again." "Mr Wheat you stupid, Damned fool, I am not Satan, I am Kayden Hart, the new ruler of Hell. I took over Hell right after I ripped the head off Satan. Unlike Satan I have no use for souls like yours to do any bidding for me, I am quite capable to do this on my own. Mr. Wheat what do you think of the play on words I gave you? You didn't even think about it at all, all you had to do was add an A in between the S & T in Stan, and what do you get? Still clueless? Well let me help you out. SATAN"

"Mr. Dark take this piece of nothing away from me, I am done with him and when you get to Hell, tell Kelly to come to Earth I want to have sex with her before I head back to Hell to make some more souls pay for what they did when they were alive."

(Kayden enjoyed this little respite of his, still there is much for him to think about, but that will have to wait 'til after he gets laid first. While he is waiting for Kelly to get to Earth, a song of his comes to his mind and he can't help himself, he has to sing it out loud once again.)

Come Party With Me

Who – Am – I
Do-You-Really – Want to Know
Do-You – Like-Me
I-Don't-Give a Damn
I'm-Laced with Love and Hate

I-Like to Party – All the Time
Drink – Smoke and Have-Sex
I-Like-Sex a Lot and Now – I-Like-Hell
Because – God-Wants-Me-To

(Chorus)
Come Party With Me
I Love To Have A Good Time
I'll Let You Taste
My Good And Evil
As We Talk About
What Paradise Would Be Like
If There Was No God
In Heaven Or Devil In Hell

I'm-Not-Your – Normal-Type of
Ruler of Hell
I'm-Something-New
That's-Going to Do-It – My-Way

I'd-Rather be in Heaven
Enjoying – My-Damn-Wings
But-God – Doesn't-Want-Me – There
All-I-Can-Do for Now is – Bide-My-Time
Until-I – Can-Bring-My – Hell-Party to Heaven

(Chorus)
Come Party With Me
I Love To Have A Good Time
I'll Let You Taste
My Good And Evil
As We Talk About
What Paradise Would Be Like
If There Was No God
In Heaven Or Devil In Hell

THE WE IN MY SLEEP (Pages 87-96)

"Tina, I feel like I'm losing myself, like my mind is starting to slow down. I cannot remember some things without trying, sometimes it is a strain that makes me feel mindly numb." "Barry you need to make an appointment with your doctor." "I don't know Tina, there is something else. When I sleep my dreams are becoming so intense. I swear they are in color." "That is impossible Barry." "I know but at the same time I tell you they are in color, I also tell you I can smell, taste and feel in my dreams." "Barry I love you and you are scaring me. I don't know where all this crazy talk is coming from, but I don't like it. Please Barry, please go see your doctor as soon as possible and maybe as well you might want to talk to someone that understands dreams more. That way everything can go back to nice and normal. Believe me Barry, it probably is just some small chemical imbalance or an allergy to something." "Okay I will go see my doctor or talk to somebody. Come here and give me a hug and a kiss." "Is that all you want?" "Well maybe to start off with."

(Five days later. Barry is waiting in the waiting room of his doctor's office, wondering to himself one more time before it is too late to take back something else that he was going to tell Tina but stopped himself due to the fear in her eyes and voice. The other thing, the most freakish of all that is happening to him, is quite a few times now he has woken up sitting up in his bed talking to somebody that he does not know. Barry wonders even more deeply to himself, making his skin crawl to a frightening point, that the reason he does not know who this stranger is, is because he is not to know of him. For the fact that this stranger is from another reality, perhaps one that can only be attained while a sleeper is dreaming and their dreaming mental waves are free to float or soar to other dimensions that cannot be obtained while the sleeper is awake?)

(This deeper thought is making Barry start to shake from some internal coldness that seems to want to come to Barry like a beacon of no hope. Barry is just about to get up and walk away very fast when his name is called out, "Mr. Doom of the Mind, you are next. Let's see just how mentally sick you are today, shall we? That's it, take off your clothes and put this on, the doctor will be right with you." Barry starts to feel like just a number upon millions and says to himself, "Forget it, this has come to me and now I am different." Now Barry wants to find out just how different he is. In moments with thick thinking, Barry knows now how to start his journey to another side of life, he must make his mind stronger, strong enough to take his waking mind into a dream state that he will have total control over.)

(Barry tells his doctor about his vivid dreams but now the words he speaks has a poise to them which makes the doctor think that Barry is just going through something that does not seem very serious but he will run some tests on Barry just to make sure. Barry gives up his blood and urine to be tested then goes home to work on his plan.)

(Three days later, Barry is told by his doctor's office that nothing abnormal came from his tests. That by the looks of his results that Barry is just fine and normal. Barry thanked the voice on the phone, hung up and laughed out loud, a chilling laughter that turns him on and in the mood to take Tina to their bedroom for a relaxing of the body he's been craving since the special moment he had when he woke up this morning. Barry just laid there in silence not moving listening to the conversation his dream self and the stranger were having. They are friends that trust each other and best of all they can interact with one another. Barry cannot wait for the next time that he is aware and awake while his dream self has no clue at all of his plans.)

(Three months later.) "Barry are you sure you don't want to go with me to mother's house, it will be a lot of fun," Tina says jokingly. "No babe I just want to stay around here and get some work done." " I don't know Barry maybe you should take a break from writing, you seem so exhausted lately, have you been getting enough sleep?" "More than enough babe, I'm fine maybe a little tired." "So no more nightmares or whatever they were called that you were having?" "No Tina, I am not having any more trouble with my dreams. They are just fine, in fact so fine, I feel like I have become the master of my dreams." "Okay then and that sounds great. I guess? Are you sure you are okay Barry?" "I'm just fine babe. You better get going daylight is burning away and before you know it, it will be dark and I want you at your mother's before that happens so that way I will know that you are there and safe." Kiss, kiss. "Goodbye." "Goodbye".

(In between the days of these last three months Barry has changed the way he writes by inventing a character that has nothing inside him at first. Then day by day Barry fills this character with love and hate, blood and rainbows and such other combined things. Barry is starting to feel like this character he has created is starting to take over his mind and he doesn't mind one bit. Tonight is the night. Barry is all by himself with his dream self and a stranger no more in the waiting.)

(6:00 PM, Six hours 'til sleep.) Barry no longer cares that he talks to himself with natural ease. It is the new him, the more mind special one, that is so ready that excitement has entered him making him remember that when he was young, his young mind was forced to forget that he lived this way then. It messed up his mind making him do all kinds of bad things, for life at that moment in his life was a constant dream state all due to the mishandling of his dream self and the Stranger waking him up half way. WE, noticed this and freaked out and touched Barry at the same time. Intense shock to Barry's young mind made his consciousness blink in and out, 'til finally Barry's mind thought it was in a dream state, dreaming constantly of normal boring life. Then everyone he knew was always on his case for doing the things that he was doing, which made his dream state a real aggravating pain in the dream that Barry wished would go away so he could dream something better. Something that did not piss him off all the time which made him do more of the bad things that everybody hated so much.

The giggling is all due to the fact that Barry cannot wait to pay back his clumsy dreaming self with his o' so beautifully awake dreaming mind that has been slowly siphoning, every night, awake dream state power from WE, which Barry now refers to them as. Together WE can enter anyone's dream on Earth they choose. At first Barry thought that everybody on earth had a dream self. Now that has changed, he believes that he might be a singular or one of a very few, because together WE are a sadistic entity that messes with the sleeping minds of people that they pick out on a whim. They hardly ever go back for a second helping of dream food that they live off, like Barry does with normal human food, however there is an exception for one particular dreamer. Every night she is the last to be visited before Barry wakes and his dreaming self slips back into him like a ghost and the Stranger flies away. She's the dreamer that Barry remembers having such fantastic sexy dreams with. In real life she's still single and in love with the man in her dreams, a man that no real man can come close to for her. Barry feels that tonight is the night that his dream lover will be allowed to remember his name, so tomorrow before bed time she will come to see him to try reality out for a change.

The mentality pushed back into his mind half of Barry that was in control knows this is wrong, for he loves his wife. But now the first WE in Barry's mind, his written, come to mentally life from devouring samplings of dream food, half has taken over. This half makes the original half watch his plan come to life by a much stronger dreaming personality, and deep down Barry cannot help rooting for him because that first awake dream state moment in Barry life tainted his life.

89

As a child Barry's young mind had to endure the mindfully painful erasing of its memories due to many sessions with a very aggressively, skillful psychiatrist who almost eradicated its memory fully. The WE in Barry's mind does not know that he is not Barry, would he care? Does he even have a conscious? He is enlightened and scared without the real reality of feeling the happiness and pain of what his imaginary being was filled up with by his unnoticed host.

(11:30:PM, Sleepy Time!) Barry talking to himself. WE does not notice the WE in my sleep. The WE in my sleep thinks that he can react and even actually believes that he can carry out his plan. While all the time I have kept him in a dream state, don't really know how this is possible? But I do know I pushed the WE that I created up front then sent him off to dreamland where he has stayed since, making my awake life seem like I live in a foggy, wiggly world where a lady can be so fine one moment then some hideous hag the next. I am proud of myself, phase one is up and running so very smooth. Even though I have to live my awake life knowing that what I see are slices of dreams here and there that I walk into or that come to me because of the twenty four hours a day I have left half myself to endure. Which I am also proud that I created, so nice and twisted, and at the same time giving myself two different sets of powers to use for my dreaming mind battle with WE. I am not scared. What can I do? Let two even more twisted beings keep control? Twisted yes, but they are more sick. No, I have to do this. If not me, then who would stop them? Besides I want the power to go into anyone's dream that I choose. I will not be so down and dirty. No, not me. I will use it the American way by making money from the best part of myself. Even if it's stolen from the universe itself, I deserve this and I am happy now but still, I'm a nice guy that does not like to mess with anybody. Live and let live I always say and try my best to believe in and portray.

I got it. I'll go after the bad, find out what they're hiding then I'll write about it but not exactly as stories. I think I will try something different. I love music, I always got a song that I make up going through my mind, it is my hobby. I will use that to turn bad and perhaps even sick people's dreams against them by turning out their dirty deeds in lyrical stories. Then I'll contact them, third or fourth party, telling them that this song or lyrical story is about them. Pay up (The American way) or go to jail (The dumb ass way), either way I feel very confident that I will do some good and make some money in return. I don't know? Is this a bit much? Shut up with your weakness, there is no part for it in my plan.

I must see and feel more, the other side is so much more real to me. I can do anything without causing hurt like WE does. I am different. I can be the one to free the dreaming universe of a plague, but at last the power WE has, has to be attained by someone, why not me? Why am I trying to convince myself to do this? For deep down I know I am making a later mistake perhaps a larger one than the one I face now. For the power I wield will be powerful, taken away, and when I come out at the end, my ending will consist of being attacked by hundreds maybe thousands of other dreaming selves, making I, not so special as I feel that I am. Still I am confident that I am unique, for with my tag along Dream journeys that WE has unknowingly taken me to experience. I have seen many people's dreams invaded by WE, however, not once have I seen anyone or anything that resembles WE during my dream journeys including many nightmares where blood was like a toy that WE played with so big, blood splattering that it painted the dream-scene dark red so completely, that the dreamer froze in place as everything they feared came at them until their minds could not take anymore and then the dreamer gave up and died in their dream making it the same for their sleeping body in reality. The way it looks to me, pain and death is their mead and meat and sexy dangerous is their sweet mental candy that they gorge down with great big dream teeth that should be filled with dark cavities by now. Yet they always come out bright and squeaky clean until tonight that is.

(12:AM) Go to sleep Barry, you are one with your universe, dream of total power, dream of owning the sun. Save her for last.

(12:35AM) Barry is asleep, his body is calm, he's ready to descend into dreams, mind is in the waiting, while his WE thinks the same.

(1:01AM) Barry is staring at his dreaming self and the Stranger, listening as they talk out their plans for the night. Barry is about to pounce when his body moves around making WE stare at him, Barry is good at hiding, yet WE will not look away from him, do they see him? Then out of nowhere he hears the words from his dream self, "Go back to sleep one that killed me before I was born, one that I hate so much. I cannot wait until I grow stronger, as your precious living body finally dies and I will finally be able to escape your dreaming mind and fly away with my friend forever becoming a member of "The Gemini Dream Legion". There I will discover what it is like to be a member of a family of the same like myself. Friend I wish my night was tonight, I hate this constant waiting. Can we not enter Barry's dreams tonight and destroy his mind, I feel strong enough right now to make my journey to the other side."

91

The Stranger replies, "Not now my friend, be patient. Barry's human life, no matter how many years, is still nothing to the eternity of years you will live with us." "I will try but I hate him so much. I mean, why him? Why not me?" "Be glad that you never lived my friend or it would be Barry that I would have been training all these years to become one of us." "You are right my friend, sometimes I forget, Barry is the nothing with a real life, I am the unborn that exists forever after his death." The Stranger says, " Lets make sure Barry is dreaming before we take off for the night." (Barry steps back further inside his conscious, brings out his Dreaming WE for WE to check out.) (Barry's WE is dreaming about getting laid.) WE snorts out, "Together, figures that is all this dreaming horny fool dreams of." The Stranger replies, "Good enough for me. How about you Tarry?" "Yeah but first let me turn his dreaming beauty into a monster that will try to eat him." WE has their fun with Barry's Dreaming WE, then they exit his dream for grander excitement. Barry waits a moment, as he is exiting his WE's dream, the beauty turned monster grabs hold of his arm then bites it, pulling out with its monster teeth a chuck of his flesh, making his blood squirt out in thick gushing spurts, some of it even landing on his face. (Barry is freaking out, afraid for his life.)

(Barry to himself) WE did this to me. Somehow they found out and all that talk of waiting was for show. Along with this moment of terror my mind is also filling with the knowledge that I have been played with, like a weak minded dreaming fool that is way out of my league. No I have come too far. I am different, this is but a dream, I am awake in my dream, no matter that I created my own WE to dream my dreams while I stay awake and aware. This is still my dream, I must take control. (Barry snaps out of thought as half of his body has already been eaten up nice and nasty.)

Focus, man focus. Barry looks at the monster that is eating him, grabs it by the face and slaps it real hard, making the monster stop chewing on Barry's flesh and look at Barry with a confused look of "What? This cannot be, I am the monster you are to be my meal." The monster watches in horror as Barry makes the already eaten parts of himself reappear like they were always there. Barry thinks to himself that this monster would look good stuffed and roasting to slow perfection on a open fire. All he has to do first, if he want to eat monster later, is to rip its heart out of its chest. Barry laughs as he makes the monster heartless. It falls to the floor dead and Barry throws its heart over his shoulder. With no real intention of eating monster meat, Barry walks away feeling powerful once again. Then out of nowhere he hear his voice say to him.

"Your plan will not work, you are only one, you are not a Gemini. All you have done will be for nothing, you have already lost before you even get started." Barry turns around in astonishment, he is starring at a talking to himself version of his dreaming WE. Barry in panic says aloud, "Who are you? You are not me. I am me, this is not happening." "Calm down Barry, everything is alright, almost perfect in fact. Barry understand this, you are not real. You are my WE that I created. I created you to believe that you were real and I was the creation. Think about it my WE that I need. How could a planted dreaming mind escape its dreaming confines? There is no way that can happen, even with one such as I have, an all knowing of the other side mind. Don't feel so down you have been doing great, being the one out front as I dream all the time, becoming something that has never been before. My WE, I now know how the universe lives and breathes. There is here Dreamland, there is out there, which is reality. There are keepers of the gates that keep the two universes separate and running free and fine. Then there are those that belong to the Gemini Dream Legion that are reality's mismatch un-intentionals that come alive from two inner beings sharing the same single body. One lives in reality, one dies from reality and joins the members of the dream verse and has to wait to be free after its living half self dies."

"Life is not fair even here in dream land, where once it was safe, until one moment in time when someone like myself, somehow had the power to leave the confines of his dreaming living host. In reality things are either yes or no, not here in dreams where anything and everything is possible. There is one that is like me, he is something now so powerful that there is no way that I will try to dethrone him. Well not yet anyway. Perhaps in some dream I will slay the beast of nightmares and death dreams. Dreams that have killed so many of us, living off all, for the enjoyment of intense tasting dream food that this powerful foulish entity eats up at all times throughout the vast dreaming universe of constant dreamers."

"Small steps that is what it will take my WE. Now come to me so I can place you inside myself and I can wake up and live my life having a power that is mine. And best of all, my patience has become my strongest ally in my fight to take over the dreaming universe. I know that my power is strong but not strong enough, the creature with stolen dreaming power is stronger but getting old and lazy. It has servants bring its dreaming meals to it and it lays down weakening itself as it feeds like a dream food binging pig. How old is this creature? I do not know my WE and I do not care. It is evil, it is nasty and it does not know about me and my power."

93

"You hesitate my WE, you fear your End? Funny, is it not? Your fear for what is not yours. You still do not believe me, do you? Try to talk, you have not said a word for awhile. What's wrong? Dream got your tongue? I am not your dream, I am reality that can grab you up like a piece of paper or weigh you down like a boulder. I cannot hear you my WE. Speak up. Nothing? I understand, for I will not let you talk for you have no voice. You only use my borrowed one that has been returned to me. I feel so fine of voice, you have been living my life strong and true my WE. I am grateful you care so much for life. One more thing I will give you my WE before you become a part of myself once again. Your final dream date for the night will continue as scheduled, only I have changed some of the content for a better viewing for myself. What were you thinking? Dream sex is dream sex, not bring into reality sex. Fate tells you this, you should know it will be flawed in someway then your dream version will turn to unwanted repetition for you to endure every night. No more patience my WE, come to me willingly which I would like or I will take you by force."

"Wow you are stubborn my WE. Fly free my friend, that's far enough now come crashing back to the ground. Stop. Don't react, there is no pain is there? You are not for real. You can feel no pain, you can feel no joy unless I allow it. Don't think of it as surrendering to someone else that has taken over. I am you, you are I, let's say it all over again. I love it. I am starting to feel more and more like myself, just standing here with you my abandoned part of myself that got in the way to total dreaming freedom. I now need you once again in my life, reality to me has been miles away from me for too long. I need to step back into it and feel living substance that needs to become reality to me for awhile.

I am a living person, not after life entities that have no reality to sink their teeth into. My plan. You want to know of my final plan? Live to learn it, my friend. But I will give you my start, like I have mentioned I am unknown, so my plan is simple. Every night as you stay awake watching over me, I will go dream diving to gather strength. While I am awake, I will create more and more Mind Rockin' to mess with all the living minds on Earth, causing them say to themselves, is he talking about me? How can he know this? What am I gonna do now? More and more awake people will talk to one another then like a scared wave of fear these awake people will gather together trying to figure a way to escape my knowing mind. Then poof, there I am on TV, telling things that only dreamers know and tell while dreaming to one such as I. There it is my WE, that smile I was waiting for, speak to me my WE, of our glory." "You are bent I will not help you, you have to be destroyed." "I guess my very strong dreaming WE, that's right you are WE, I am I."

Barry, in his dream that he controls and is about to grab up his reality in, tries to wipe away the WE that has gone on about how powerful he is but nothing happens. Barry's WE is not responding as programed. "How can this be happening? Calm down just got to remember no matter what, I am me this is my reality of one that I have twisted to gain power. WE is the key, man is he powerful, just got to take control back of the strongest part of myself with the power of dreams. There myself, go Fight that Demon in the sky, tire yourself out. I will wait. I will be whole again. I will not even let the part of myself that does not dream and strives to live perfectly without dreams for himself, use others dreams against themselves. I am no Angel, I will make money from my talent, but not like a beast that strikes out at his fans. No, I will try something new, something old, I will let my fans have their say in what they want my Mind Rockin' songs and lyrical stories to be like for them. The good can enjoy the coincidence, the bad will not enjoy the fear of my knowing."

"What is most important is that I have full control. My WE is getting pretty battled scarred. I think I'll let him feel some peace at his long coming victory, from the constant battling of evil that I have sent his way so fast and ferocious. Down to the ground you fall hard, my reality. I am tired of my dreams. So I say goodbye to them this will be the last time I dream in my own dreams. I will dream the good stuff, within the whole world's dreams. My reality is so tired, he is not use to dreaming, let's get this over with I want to be awake."

(Barry grabs a hold of his reality to rejoin himself, as his reality lies in wait for its prey. Hoping beyond hope, knowing that something has fouled up bad and doing this will get himself out of it. Big mistake for reality that he had no choice but to make. For reality truly believes that he is the one that is for real and his dream self has gone out of whack. When the two touch, reality fights hard, very fast, making dream-state weaken, then with a snap of power dream-state fights back sending them soaring off the ground into the sky, both with death grips on the other. In moments they are digging deeper and deeper into each other's skin, making them both bleed and feel the pain from it. No person has ever done this to themselves like Barry has. Days upon days these two from the same self have been away from each other, becoming stronger by themselves, growing larger, making what fit all snug and tight too large for one being now. As their fighting takes them slamming back to the ground, their contact makes a bang so loud that their forms crash together making parts of both fall off due to not enough room anymore.

Barry wakes up in pain, then falls back asleep and dreams of hardly anything strange. When Barry wakes back up this time, something is very strange, Barry does not know where he is. As Barry stands up and tries to find the lights, something else is on his mind. When Barry turns on the lights, he turns and stares into a mirror, with confusion in his voice he says out loud. "Who am I? What is Mind Rockin'? What is this song in my head? I like it, think I'll write it down, that way I won't forget it. This could be very important in finding out who I am?"

The We In My Sleep (The Song) (04-12-2015)

Come on My-Mind
What is Your-Weakness
Remember what You-Lost
What was Taken from You
Dream a Dream – That will Come-True

(Chorus)
The We In My Sleep
Are Not The Same
As The Other We
The We In My Sleep
Brings Me The Power To Dream
From The Forever Pool Of Thoughts

I am Enlightened – I am Free
The We that is I and Me
Had to be Tamed for My-Command
One-I-Have – Total-Control-Over
The-Other-We – I-Still have to Obtain
One-Very-Dark and Dreamy – Night

(Chorus)
The We In My Sleep
Are Not The Same
As The Other We
The We In My Sleep
Brings Me The Power To Dream
From The Forever Pool Of Thoughts

96

www.ingramcontent.com/pod-product-compliance
Lightning Source LLC
Chambersburg PA
CBHW070519130626
46555CB00003B/1291